ROSE CAMPION

and the

STOLEN SECRET

Also by
LYN
GARDNER

Olivia's First Term
Olivia Flies High
Olivia and the Movie Stars
Olivia's Enchanted Summer
Olivia and the Great Escape
Olivia's Winter Wonderland
Olivia's Curtain Call

ROSE CAMPION

and the
STOLEN SECRET

LYN GARDNER

nosy
crow

First published in the UK in 2016 by Nosy Crow Ltd
The Crow's Nest, 10a Lant Street
London, SE1 1QR, UK

www.nosycrow.com

ISBN: 978 0 85763 486 3

Nosy Crow and associated logos are trademarks and/or
registered trademarks of Nosy Crow Ltd

A CIP catalogue record for this book will be available from the
British Library.

Printed and bound in the UK by Clays Ltd, St. Ives Plc
Typeset by Tiger Media

Papers used by Nosy Crow are made from wood grown in
sustainable forests.

1 3 5 7 9 10 8 6 4 2

For Hector
L.G.

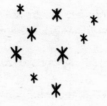

1

Thirty-two years before our story starts

The unlined wooden coffin had been placed on the great dining table of Easingford Hall. The coffin maker stepped back to allow the new Lord of Easingford, Henry Edgar Easingford, to approach the open coffin. His eyes midnight dark, Lord Henry placed the tiny corpse of his nephew, Edward, into the coffin, next to the body of the child's dead mother, Lily.

The baby was still tightly swaddled in the fine linen sheet that the midwife had wrapped him in before she'd handed him to his uncle. Henry had taken the crying child to his own chamber, and there, away from prying eyes, he'd gazed for a moment at the tiny butterfly birthmark on the back of his nephew's neck that marked him out as an Easingford child. Then he had picked up a feather bolster and pressed it over the child's face.

Now Lord Henry placed a blue ribbon and a small silver cup engraved with the family name and butterfly crest into the coffin. This burial might be hasty, but tradition dictated that no Easingford should be buried without a reminder that he or she was part of a great and noble family, rich enough to bury silver with their dead.

The coffin was made of elm, not the polished oak that the coffin maker knew it should be. Poor Lady Lily had been a great heiress in her own right, and her tiny baby son, Edward, would have been the new Lord Easingford had he lived. But a polished oak coffin took time to make and Lord Henry was in a hurry to bury his brother's wife and newborn son.

The coffin maker, Joe, kept his head bowed respectfully, but he wondered what the baby's father, Frederick Edward, the previous Lord Easingford and Henry's identical twin brother, would have made of such indecent haste. But Frederick Easingford had been laid into the cold ground a mere six months previously after an accident while out riding with his brother.

Lord Henry claimed that the influenza epidemic sweeping the county meant the dead had to be buried quickly and their infection buried with them. Even now the horse and carriage stood harnessed on the curved drive in front of the remote house, ready to convey the coffin to the moorland church where the parson, Oliver Dorset Woldingham, was waiting to conduct the funeral service.

Lily had been Oliver's rich cousin. Village gossip said that Oliver, who was poorer than the mice in his own church, had been in love with her.

Joe looked uneasily at his wife, Abigail, the village midwife. She brought children into the world; he helped people on their way out. But not these kinds of people. Not the gentry. Everything about it felt wrong. It was as if Lord Easingford wanted to wipe away all evidence of his sister-in-law and nephew as soon as he could. The corpses of mother and babe were barely cold.

The Hall was almost deserted: most of the servants had been dismissed over a week ago, with the influenza epidemic cited as the reason. Only the cook, the under-maid and a stable boy had been retained to care for Lily Easingford and her younger sister, Sarah Dorset. Sarah was an orphan of sixteen, who had come to live with Lily after the death of their father, Lord Dorset. When Lily's husband died, Sarah had become Henry's ward. Like Lily, she was reputed to have a great fortune of her own.

When she had first come to live at Easingford last year, Joe had spotted her out on the moor several times, dancing and running and jumping as if she were still a small child. Her voice had carried as sweetly as a curlew's. Some in the village disapproved, considering her behaviour to be unladylike, but Joe didn't. He liked to see a young girl as full of life as the moor itself. Recently he had stumbled across her weeping in a blaze of heather, and she had risen like a startled golden plover and fled, but not before he had seen a livid red mark on her cheek.

Everyone in the village knew that the doctor had called on her ladyship yesterday. Cook said he had shaken his head and said that unless the baby came quickly the mother would be dead of influenza before it could be born. Then the doctor had fallen sick and been too ill to attend either the dawn birth or the death that had

4

followed before the milky sun was fully risen. It was now just lunchtime.

Abigail had been sent to tend her ladyship as she gave birth. She had been collected from the village by the stable boy in a cart after midnight, and they had trundled on the track across the moor under a moon of beaten silver. The labour was already far advanced, the mother sinking fast. Abigail knew she should have been called earlier.

The coffin maker could see from his wife's stiff back and the way she bit her lip that she was unhappy. Unhappy and frightened. By the unseemly haste to bury the dead. By his lordship's grim-set face. By the headstone that was already being carved by the stonemason to mark the passing of "Lady Lily Easingford and her stillborn son, Edward Frederick Dorset Easingford". Most of all she was unhappy and frightened by the word "stillborn".

"That bairn was alive, bonny and bawling, when I swaddled him," she had insisted over and over to her husband, pacing restlessly as he had hammered the coffin together behind the stables. "There was nothing to be done for her ladyship. All the doctors in the land could not have saved her, but the babe breathed, I know he did. His lordship only had him a few minutes alone and that's when the breath went out of him."

The coffin maker put a finger to her lips. It did no good to make trouble. Not if they wanted to go on living in Easingford, the Yorkshire village where he had been born and generations had been born before him. Besides, the child was well and truly dead now. Babies did die. It was the way of the world.

Abigail knew that, more than most. She had given birth to five babies and not a single one had survived for more than a few days. Joe had made the five little coffins himself, and laid their tiny bodies inside, the last just a few days previously. All Abigail wanted was a child to look after and love but there would be no more babies. It was unfair, but the world cared nothing for fairness.

Joe watched Lord Henry as he looked into the coffin. His lordship's face was composed in an aspect of sorrow, but his eyes – cold, dark and unwelcoming – said something else. With a jolt, the coffin maker realised that his lordship wasn't unhappy that this mother and child were dead. He was pleased. Lord Henry couldn't quite control the tiny smirk of triumph that played at the corners of his mouth, a smirk that said *I'm head of the Easingford dynasty at last, lord of all I survey*.

Joe shivered. Maybe Abigail was right when she said that the bairn had been born blooming and healthy. He lowered his head further in case Lord Easingford saw in his eyes what the coffin maker knew. Knowledge could be a dangerous thing. It could get you killed.

"It's time," said his lordship curtly. "Hammer the lid down. Then bring the coffin to the carriage. I'll send the stable boy to help you lift it."

The coffin maker slid the elm lid into place and began to nail it shut with the *tack, tack, tack* tattoo that marked every death. Lord Henry pressed a guinea into the coffin maker's hand and strode away. The coffin maker and his wife both knew they were being paid to keep quiet. It was blood money.

The last nail was being tapped into the lid when they both heard something. The coffin maker turned silk-pale and dropped his hammer; Abigail put her hand to her mouth, a circle of surprise. There it was again – a sound no louder than the mew of a kitten. It was unmistakably coming from the coffin.

Joe started to tear at the coffin nails with the claw of the hammer, his fingers trembling. He peeled off the elm lid, and he and Abigail looked down into the coffin. The baby's blue eyes stared back at them as if astonished. For a tiny moment it seemed as if the baby smiled at them. Abigail lifted the babe from the coffin and put him in the crook of her arm where he fitted perfectly. The baby snuffled against her, his breathing shallow but certain. Abigail adjusted the linen swaddling cloth, her fingers grazing one of the tiny, almost invisible butterflies stitched into each corner of the sheet.

"We must tell his lordship," Joe said, his voice hoarse with surprise and terror.

"No," said Abigail quickly. "That's the last thing we should do if we want this baby to live. We must take him, keep little Edward safe. Far away from here."

"You would make us child snatchers," her husband said quietly.

"We'll be murderers else," she replied, fixing him with her steely gaze until he was forced to look away.

"We'll be denying him his birthright," said Joe.

"We'll be giving him his life. Do you think he would survive more than a few hours here unprotected?"

"We'll have to leave Easingford. Leave our whole lives behind."

"We'll go to London. Disappear into the crowd."

Time was running out. They could hear the stable boy's heavy tread in the hall. Joe nodded at Abigail, who put the baby in her basket and left the room, heading below stairs to the kitchen where she could slip out of the back door. Joe reached into the coffin and stuffed the ribbon and tiny silver cup in his pocket.

"God and your ladyship forgive me," he whispered. He quickly began hammering the lid back into place. "We'll keep him safe. I promise."

Joe and the stable boy hoisted the coffin. It was light, as if her ladyship's bones were made of feathers. They carried it carefully to the door, out into the hall and through the vast stone doorway of Easingford Hall to the carriage.

When they'd left, the great dining room was

as silent as an empty church. Then a girl crept from behind the thick damask curtains. She was dressed all in black, mourning for her sister. Her pale face was scoured with tears.

"Sarah! Sarah! We are ready for the church." Lord Henry was calling her.

The girl's eyes darkened with fear and her hands trembled. She slipped towards the door that led to the kitchen stairs, opened it quietly and vanished. A few minutes later she reappeared at the front of the house, her eyes downcast.

"There you are, girl. You have kept us all waiting. Get in the carriage and show some respect for your dead sister."

Sarah's eyes blazed; two peony spots blossomed on her cheeks. "When did you ever show her any respect, Henry?" she hissed.

His lordship seized her by the wrist and dragged her towards the leading carriage where Joe and the stable boy waited. Henry pushed her into the carriage and slammed the door shut, and then he walked around to the other side. The stable boy ran to open the door for him.

The window where Sarah sat was slightly open. Sarah looked directly at the coffin maker.

"You and your wife are good people," she said. "The secret is safe with me. God protect you and my nephew, Edward." She spoke so softly that nobody else could have heard.

Joe's stomach lurched. The girl knew what he and Abigail had done. As soon as the carriage and the cart disappeared, he gathered his tools quickly and strode across the moor towards the village as fast as he could. Before the Reverend Oliver Dorset Woldingham had concluded the funeral service, Joe and Abigail had set off for London with the rightful Lord of Easingford sleeping peacefully in a basket, little dreaming of how lucky he was to be alive.

Rose Campion leaned out of the dormitory window on the top floor of Miss Pecksniff's Academy for Young Ladies and gave the drainpipe a hard tug. It was safely secured to the wall. Rose's hands still smarted from where Miss Pecksniff had brought down the ruler on her palms, delivering each blow with a gleam in her eye that suggested she was enjoying herself immensely and only regretted that she hadn't given Rose a really good beating sooner.

Rose and Miss Pecksniff had been at war from the moment Rose had arrived at the Notting Hill school. Her mop of unruly conker-coloured hair, slate-dark eyes and unladylike rosy cheeks seemed to instantly annoy the head teacher.

Her ink-blotched pinafore (she'd been trying to write a song for her music-hall act in the hansom cab on her way to the school) was the final straw. Miss Pecksniff had stared appalled as Rose, glimpsing the velvety-green lawn, gave a whoop of joy, leapt from the still-moving hansom, ran on to the grass and turned a cartwheel. Rose had never seen a flourishing patch of grass, let alone a lawn, in muddy Southwark. It was perfect for practising cartwheels.

"Come here at once!" said Miss Pecksniff, her voice like an angry wasp and her pale-blue eyes bulging in horrified astonishment. "Young ladies never turn cartwheels and they are never, in any circumstances, permitted to walk on the grass."

"Why ever not?" asked Rose cheerily, genuinely interested.

"Because I say so!" snapped Miss Pecksniff.

Rose was surprised. Whenever she asked a question of her guardian, Thomas Campion, owner of Campion's Palace of Varieties and Wonders, he always tried to answer it, even though recently he had said that Rose had more questions than he had answers for and the only solution was to send her to school.

Rose was clever enough to know that the war with Miss Pecksniff was one she could never win. She'd made a promise to Thomas that she would stay at school, as he wanted, for at least a year, and she never broke her promises. Well, only if it was really necessary.

Rose knew that Thomas was only trying to do his best for her. He'd been trying to do that every day since the summer's morning almost thirteen years ago when he'd found her, just a tiny babe, wrapped in half a threadbare linen sheet by Campion's stage door. Rose was always eager to hear the story. But Thomas found it hard to talk about; he'd lost his wife and infant twin daughters to the measles just weeks before.

Thomas had raised her as a daughter, taught her to read and write – both of which she picked up with astonishing ease – encouraged her to perform at Campion's and given her an enduring love of Shakespeare. Thomas said the playwright was a genius and Rose agreed. Rose dreamed of one day starring at the Lyceum or the Haymarket, and dazzling theatregoers with her Rosalind from *As You Like It* or Viola from *Twelfth Night*.

She loved Thomas and Campion's fiercely

but she still liked to imagine that when she became the most famous actress on the London stage the mother who'd abandoned her would at last come and claim her as her own. She enjoyed visualising over and over in her head the tearful and deeply moving moment when they were finally reunited and her mother begged her forgiveness.

Thomas told her that if she was going to be a great actress she needed to see a bit of life. Thomas hoped that school would give Rose a glimpse of a different world from the rough and tumble of life at the music hall on the south side of the Thames. Campion's was a well-known landmark situated down Hangman's Alley on what some whispered to be an old plague pit. Everyone said it was haunted. Hardly a day went by without one of the ballet girls claiming to have glimpsed a stranger's face behind hers in the dressing-room mirror or to have seen an apparition of a lady in grey staring down at her from the otherwise empty gallery.

Such claims made Rose scoff. She didn't believe in ghosts. Ghosts were about death, and Rose was full of life. Although she looked like an angel – albeit an often slightly grubby one – she could be a right little devil who thought nothing of hitching up her skirts if it helped her run faster, or giving the Tanner Street boys a mouthful if she caught them trying to sneak into Campion's without paying. Seeing how bright she was, Thomas wanted Rose to have thebenefit of a proper education; unfortunately, the hefty fees charged by Miss Pecksniff fooled him into thinking her establishment would provide one.

Rose knew that this other world, with its elocution and deportment lessons, and the gossipy young ladies who looked down their little snub noses at Rose, was not for her. She belonged at Campion's. She rubbed her fingers that still bore the indentation of the sharp edge of Miss Pecksniff's ruler and angrily remembered the head teacher's words from that morning.

"That one," Miss Pecksniff had snarled, bringing the ruler down as hard as she could, "is for always questioning my authority." Miss Pecksniff's exertions had made tendrils of hair escape from her bun so it looked as if her thin, pinched face was surrounded by tiny dancing worms. Her pale-blue eyes were feverish.

Thwack. Thwack. Rose shut her eyes but refused to flinch. *Thwack.* She bit the inside of her cheek. She would not be broken by Miss Pecksniff.

"That one is because you don't belong here with decent, well-bred girls," shouted Miss Pecksniff, her fury rising at Rose's lack of tears, "and this one is because Thomas Campion does not pay his bills."

Rose opened her eyes wide. She was shocked. If there was one thing that Thomas always did, it was pay his debts. It was a matter of honour.

"You're lying," shouted Rose, and to Miss Pecksniff's astonishment she grabbed the ruler out of her hand and broke it clean in half. Miss Pecksniff shrieked loudly as other members of staff came rushing to her aid. The handyman, Jarvis, was a great burly man who grabbed Rose and pulled her arms behind her back, holding her wrists roughly.

"She's like a wild animal!" cried Miss Pecksniff. "Lock her in the dormitory until I've decided what to do with her!"

Miss Pecksniff longed to expel Rose but she knew she couldn't send the child home with her hands so red and raw from the beating. What she had told Rose was not entirely true:

Thomas Campion had been very late paying the current term's fees, but he had paid up, apologising profusely for the delay and even paying her interest on the money. Miss Pecksniff would decide what to do with Rose over luncheon.

* ✕ *

Rose gave the drainpipe another tug, just to be sure, then she dropped her carpet bag out of the dormitory window. It fell on to the gravel below with a crunch. Rose held her breath, fearful that somebody would hear. But nobody came, so she hitched up her skirts and scrambled on to the window sill. Taking a deep breath, she swung herself out on to the drainpipe. Despite the pain in her hands, she clung to it like a monkey and began to climb carefully down. She reached the bottom without injury, apart from a ragged tear in her knickerbockers when they caught on a nail in the brickwork. She picked up her bag and turned towards the open gates at the end of the drive. She stomped viciously across the middle of the wet lawn, leaving a very visible trail of boot marks in the manicured grass. When she reached the road she set off at a run towards Southwark.

She had been at Miss Pecksniff's Academy for exactly a year and a day. She had kept her promise. It was time to go home to Campion's.

3

Rose walked south over London Bridge through thick fog, people and animals looming out of it towards her like ghosts. One man was herding a small flock of sheep; a woman carried several squawking chickens in a wooden crate. Children ran about, begging; a chanter stood right in the middle of the bridge singing a popular song, and a tray man was hawking shrimps and cockles.

Out of habit, Rose scanned the faces of all the women who were walking towards her. She speculated that she and her mother could be passing each other at this very moment, completely unaware that they were tied by blood. She wondered whether her mother did the same, desperately searching for a resemblance in any of the girls who passed by, trying to find the daughter she had abandoned so long ago.

Rose knew she was being silly. She was still living where her mother had left her and she knew that Thomas would tell her immediately if anyone came looking for her. And besides, if her mother had wanted to find Rose, she would surely have come by now. It could only mean one of two things: either her mother didn't care about her, or she was dead. Both options were unbearable.

Rose looked down into the cold, dark Thames and shivered. Maybe her desperate mother had left her at the music hall and then promptly thrown herself in the treacherous, seething river? Or maybe she was out there somewhere in the world with another little girl of her own who she loved and cherished, and she never gave a thought to the baby she had abandoned so long ago. Rose tried not to think about that because when she did she felt a sharp pain in her throat that no amount of swallowing could dislodge.

She hurried off along the river path, looking over the wall as she did so. It was low tide and the mudlarks were out, scratching along the murky shoreline and wading into the mud, some of them up to their thighs, looking for something – anything – of value to sell. The yellow fog was patchier by the river's edge and some of the mudlark children spotted her, shouted her name and waved. She waved back, wishing she had a penny for each of them.

She ran across the road, ignoring the cries of the costermongers, coffee-stall owners and lark sellers, and dodged several barrows and carts that were clattering down the muddy street. She slipped into Hangman's Alley. Campion's Palace of Varieties and Wonders loomed out of the gathering gloom, its windows winking brightly as if welcoming her back.

She gave a little skip of excitement as she pushed open the gate to the yard and Ophelia, the theatre cat, looked up from cleaning her ears and padded over to weave in and out of Rose's legs. In the yard, the Fabulous Flying Fongolis, a troupe of five acrobat brothers from Wapping, were practising their act, the youngest brother being tossed through the air like a log by his older siblings. Madame Dubonnet, the Famous

Baritone, was warming up her voice. Rose found it amazing how such a low, deep sound came out of this young, frail woman. Rose grinned as she headed for the stage door, and Madame Dubonnet gave her a cheery wave as she passed.

"Look what the wind's blown in; if it isn't little Rosie back to try us all," grinned Jem, a Campion's regular, who was playing cards for pennies with some of the stagehands. "Come over here, Rosie, and bring me some luck." Rose smiled and shook her head. Jem was always betting and always losing. He never learned. Tomorrow he'd be trying to get Thomas to advance him his wages.

O'Leary, the ancient actor whose first name had been mislaid somewhere between leaving Dublin and arriving at Campion's, was slumped on a chair just inside the stage door. He was supposed to be on duty, but he was fast asleep and snoring, gin fumes wafting from his mouth with every exhalation. Rose took a step further into the welcoming, familiar fug of Campion's. A couple of ballet dancers, thin, pinched-looking waifs with highly rouged cheeks, were practising steps by the edge of the stage and giggling. They eyed Rose with undisguised curiosity, and Rose realised she must look a strange sight: dressed like a lady but without either bonnet or gloves.

Rose smiled at them. Joe Blow, the clog-dancing cornet man, who was waiting to do his turn on the other side of the stage, saw her and bowed, blowing her a kiss. Rose grinned at the stagehands, who were busy trying to untangle the backcloth that was used for the melodrama *The Perils of Priscilla*. It must be on the bill tonight, which Rose thought was odd because although it was a real crowd-pleaser, Thomas found its endless stabbings and shootings tasteless and gory.

She walked to the edge of the stage where Peg Leg Tony and his Amazing Dancing Collies were performing. The collies were wearing little blue velvet jackets, and ruffs around their necks, and they were running around the stage in a circle of eight. In a minute they would be up and walking backwards on their hind legs. Any act involving animals was always a sure-fire hit in the music halls. Rose had seen lions and tigers performing at the Alhambra in Leicester Square but the big cats had seemed miserable behind the bars of their cages.

Rose took a step closer to the stage and was hit by a wall of heat coming from the gaslights. She looked beyond the flickering footlights out into the hazy auditorium. It was still early, but even so she was surprised by how sparse the crowd was. She frowned. Thomas hadn't mentioned anything to her in his letters about business being bad. It must have taken a real downturn since Christmas.

She turned to go up the stairs to Thomas's study when she was enveloped in a hug from behind and a voice said, "Lor, Rosie. It's a treat to see yer." Lottie, one of the ballet girls, was squeezing her so tight she could hardly breathe. She could smell the greasepaint on Lottie's skin. Lottie had been dancing at Campion's since she was fourteen. At nineteen she was considered an old trouper, sensible and capable too.

"Hello, Lots," said Rose, beaming. "I missed you at Christmas. I was sorry to hear about your dad."

"Ta. Poor Dad would 'ave 'ad a pauper's funeral wiv nobody there at all if Thomas 'adn't paid for it and given me the train fare back to Deal. But my, ain't you a fine thing. You look and sound like a duchess, Rosie. Very la-di-da. That fancy school will make a proper lady out of you yet."

"Never," laughed Rose. "I'm home. For good."

The orchestra struck up and Lottie jumped.

"Listen, Rosie, see yer after the cancan. We can catch up while them dratted collies are doing their second turn. Can yer Adam and Eve it? Them stupid dancing mutts are more popular than us girls!" Lottie pecked Rose's cheek and turned towards the stage.

"See you later, Lots," Rose called after her. "I'm going to say hello to Thomas."

Lottie swung back round, an anxious expression on her face. "Wait, Rosie, you should know something…" But Rose had already started up the stairs and didn't hear her.

She reached the door of Thomas's office. Unusually, it was closed. Thomas always kept it open so that everyone at Campion's, whether they were top of the bill or the lowliest stagehand, could talk to him at any time, and he could always get a sense of what was happening downstairs even if he was busy with paperwork. The sounds of the cancan wafted up the stairs. It was a sound that always made

Rose want to dance.

Nose to nose with the closed office door she took a deep breath. She wasn't looking forward to explaining what had happened at Miss Pecksniff's. But she knew that he would listen to her side of the story and when he saw her raw, red hands he would believe she had been treated unjustly.

"Surprise!" she cried, pushing open the door with some force.

A strange sight met her eyes. Thomas was not alone in the room. There were four solemn-faced men seated in a circle, all dressed in black. For a moment Rose thought maybe someone had died. But then a fleeting image of vultures perched on rocks and waiting patiently to swoop on the body of a dying man came to mind. She saw Thomas's shocked and anxious face.

"Rosie! What on earth are you doing here?" he asked.

It wasn't quite the welcome she had expected. "I've come home to Campion's," said Rose.

One of the men gave a thin, cold smile, the kind a wolf might make just before it eats you.

"You'd better enjoy it while you can then," he said, "because it may not be home for long."

"What does he mean?" demanded Rose, looking imploringly at Thomas.

He stood and put an arm around her shoulders. He seemed to have suddenly aged by at least twenty years.

"I'm so sorry, Rose. I never wanted you to find out this way. Thing is, I made some investments and used Campion's as security. And now they've failed. It wouldn't matter if business was good. But it's not. Times are changing. We can't compete with the swanky West End halls any more. The Victorious and the Finch have both gone under in recent months, and if business doesn't improve so I can pay off my debts, these gentlemen from the bank will close Campion's down."

Rose felt as if she had been punched in the stomach.

"Rose, I promise I will do everything in my power to ensure that doesn't happen." Thomas sighed. "But I can't promise that I'll succeed. If business would just pick up we might stand a chance."

From downstairs Rose heard the crowd laughing at something happening on stage. But instead of feeling cheered by it, it felt as if the world was laughing at her. She glared at the four black vultures.

"You won't get your hands on Campion's," she cried. "I won't let you!"

Then she turned and marched down the stairs before they could see her burst into furious tears.

Rose sat in the auditorium facing the stage. Eager to help save Campion's, she'd offered to patch up some old costumes so they didn't need to buy new ones. She loathed sewing. She'd been at it for hours and had just decided to reread *The Winter's Tale* instead. It was one of Rose's favourite plays, not least because she identified so with Perdita, whose name meant "the lost one".

On stage, Lottie was rehearsing the ballet girls in a new dance with an Eastern theme that was all the rage. Lottie said they could use some of the costumes from the *Aladdin* pantomime they had staged the previous year so it would be cheap. High above the whirling dancers, Molly Blinder, who did acrobatic tricks while hanging by her teeth from a strap above the stage, was practising a new routine. Rose thought it looked agonising, but Molly said her act wasn't half as painful as it appeared, and that you had to work with whatever gifts you'd been given, which in her case was freakishly strong teeth.

Thomas had asked everyone at Campion's to come up with ideas to lure bigger audiences into the theatre. Lottie had suggested the new Eastern dance, preferably with added snake charmer. But another of the dancers, Tess, had squealed at the thought of having snakes in the building and Thomas said it might be quite hard to find a snake charmer in Southwark. Molly was keen on an elephant, until Thomas pointed out that finding an elephant might also be tricky, and it would be expensive to feed and impossible to fit through Campion's doorway.

"No," Rose had agreed thoughtfully, "but we could easily get a flock of sheep through it."

"Sheep?" asked Thomas, raising an eyebrow.

"Yes," said Rose. "Then we could do the sheep-shearing scene from *The Winter's Tale*. I saw a load being herded across the bridge the other day. We could borrow a few for the evening. It'd be a big crowd-puller."

"Ain't sure me collie dogs and sheep would mix," said Peg Leg Tony doubtfully.

"Ah, maybe not," agreed Thomas, recalling a nasty incident when Ophelia the cat had pounced on stage when Tansy Quilp and her Miraculous Singing Canaries were performing. Rose, who hadn't liked the canary act, said that Ophelia was clearly a very discerning critic.

A few days after the meeting, Peg Leg Tony said he'd had an offer from the Fortune in Hoxton and would be moving on at the end of the week. So Rose was determined to pursue *The Winter's Tale* idea. How hard could it be to borrow a few sheep? She put down her copy of the play and was planning to go to the bridge and find a shepherd, when she heard Thomas calling.

"Hey, Rosie. Guess who's here in my study?"

"Queen Victoria?"

"Better than that," said Thomas. "Ned Dorset! And Gracie and little Freddie. Come up. We're having tea and cakes. Ned Dorset and his family back in London is something to celebrate."

Rose rushed up the stairs and straight into the arms of a tousle-haired young man wearing a Lincoln-green waistcoat.

"Whoa, Rose," said Ned. "You nearly knocked me over!"

But Rose was already hugging Grace and then she picked up Freddie, a small cheerful boy of about seven, who had Ned's colouring and eyes but Grace's features.

Rose loved the Dorset family. Ned had arrived at Campion's just a few weeks after Rose had been found on the doorstep. Once, Ned had told her that finding the little baby had given Thomas a reason to keep living.

Ned had done a magic act at Campion's and played all the juvenile leads in the melodramas. Grace was a contortionist in a troupe of acrobats who had been passing through Campion's on their way up north. Grace hadn't gone with them. It was love at first sight and she and Ned had worked up an act together until Freddie had been born. But Ned's heart was in the theatre. He dreamed of playing Hamlet and Macbeth. Thomas had been sad to see the little family go five years before, but he had been supportive of Ned's eagerness to make his way in the theatre.

"So, Ned, my boy, how have you been?" asked Thomas.

Rose saw a quick look pass between Ned

33

and Grace and she noted how threadbare their clothes were.

"Good," said Ned, but not entirely convincingly.

Thomas frowned.

"He's played Laertes in *Hamlet* and Sebastian in *Twelfth Night*, and he has been playing Edmund in *King Lear* at Oxford," said Grace brightly.

"Good," said Thomas encouragingly.

"Yes," said Grace. "He had lovely reviews too, but then he threw up the part and said we had to come to London."

Her tone made it clear she hadn't understood, or agreed with, the decision.

Thomas turned to Ned. "So what brought you to London?"

"I had some urgent business I needed to attend to. I got a job as the villain in the panto at the Shaftesbury in Hackney," said Ned, "but it folded early and the whole place has closed down."

Thomas nodded grimly. "It's a tough time for the small halls like us. We can't compete with the spectacles at those fancy places up West."

Grace looked embarrassed. "We'd heard things were difficult here, Thomas," she said.

"Not so difficult that I can't give you and Ned a job, Gracie, if you both want one," said Thomas. "We're trying to freshen things up. You and Ned would help. I'm negotiating for another new act too, one that's not been seen in London before. Hope it will bring people in."

"Your offer is generous, Thomas," said Ned, "but if you, and my darling Grace and Freddie, could just bear with me for a week or two there's something I need to sort out first." A worried frown wrinkled his brow. "I've got to right the wrongs of the past before I look to my future."

"Well, let's have the tea and cakes," said Thomas cheerfully, and for a while the chatter was all of the halls and theatre and who was playing which roles where, although Ned was rather quiet and occasionally Rose looked up and saw him staring at her pensively. Something seemed to be bothering him.

After tea, Rose took Freddie and Grace down into the yard so Freddie could play with Ophelia.

"Is everything all right with Ned?" asked Rose.

Grace shook her head. "There's something

eating him up. But he won't tell me what it is, which makes me think it's to do with his mysterious family. He's always been a closed book as far as they're concerned. I once asked him how he could really love me if he didn't trust me enough to tell me about his past. I knew I'd hurt him but he said that he was only trying to keep me safe by not talking about his family."

"Maybe he was raised by a gang of murdering thieves and cutpurses," said Rose, thinking that would be quite exciting.

"Well, they must be very hoity-toity cutpurses," said Grace. "You can tell by the way he talks and behaves that he was raised a gentleman and had an education. I just wish he'd tell me why he ran out on that life."

"I really hope he's going to accept Thomas's offer of work," said Rose, who was delighted that Ned and his family might return to Campion's but worried that Thomas would be further stretched financially.

"It'd be a big relief," said Grace. "Where we're living in Shoreditch is grim." Then she added, "But at least it's not the workhouse. An old friend of Ned's asked him to visit one just a few days ago. It was over this way. Lor, but he said

36

it was awful."

"Who did he go to see?"

"A former chorus girl called Eliza something. Eliza Chowser? Think that was it. Said he didn't know her himself but that she had worked at the Victorious some years back and had fallen on hard times. He said the workhouse was a whimpering, shivering kind of place."

"All the more reason for you all to come back to Campion's then," said Rose cheerfully.

Grace nodded. "But it will be hard for Ned. I think he dreamed of returning to London in triumph. To the Lyceum or somewhere grand, and then inviting Thomas to come and see him. But he's not so proud that he'd let Freddie and me starve. I don't mind Shoreditch for myself. I love Ned. I'd follow him to hell and back if need be. But I'd like something better for Freddie, and I know that Ned does too."

After that they'd gone back upstairs. As they entered the study, Thomas and Ned broke off talking, but not before Rose had heard Thomas say, "Why the sudden interest in the babies, Ned, boy? You know I'm not one for reminiscing." His sad face was caught in the glow from the oil lamp. "There was so much loss around that time. Too much to bear."

Then he saw Rose standing in the doorway and brightened. "At least I've still got my Rose, and I couldn't do without her. She's been a daughter to me."

Ned smiled and stood up. "Come on, Grace, we must return to Shoreditch. I need to send a letter to America by the evening post." He turned to Thomas. "Grace and I will discuss your offer of work, Thomas. I'll be in touch. Thank you."

5

It was a week later. Lizzie Gawkin, face as plain as flour and eyes as sharp and steely as a stiletto, stepped out of the Southwark lodging house where she had arrived late the previous night. The clock of St Olave's Church struck ten. She and the Infant Phenomenon were not expected at Campion's music hall until early evening.

She drank in the bustling street, where cabs and carriages fought for space and the voices of hawkers and ballad sellers, all eager to trade their wares, competed with the yaps and barks of a pack of dogs as they fought over scraps. Ah, London. She loved it. Although of course she would prefer to be in Piccadilly rather than these stinking streets. But at last she was within the grasp of the life of luxury that she knew she'd always deserved. She just had to be very clever.

It was good to be back after all this time. Twelve, nearly thirteen years of being patient. Five years of tedium buried alive in Balham, followed by seven trailing around filthy continental music halls with the brat, and then close to a year on the northern hall circuit. Biding her time until it was safe to return to London and finally put the squeeze on Lord Henry Easingford.

She patted her pocket where she kept the torn-out page from *The Times*, dated a few weeks previously. It speculated that the Queen would shortly make Henry Easingford a privy councillor. *Now* was the moment to strike.

Lizzie needed to be in London to carry out her plan, but she would have felt safer if she'd signed a contract with a music hall north of the river. There she was less likely to be recognised as Bess Jingle, as she'd been known in her Bermondsey days. She went back to her maiden name, Gawkin, following that unfortunate incident at the Victorious when a tenor she had been blackmailing had threatened to expose her and she had been forced to shut his mouth. Permanently.

There had been quite a hue and cry over his death, and her name had been mentioned. It had got the wind up her and she'd had to flee to her sister's down Balham way. Although, of course, her first few weeks at Balham had been very enlightening. So much so, she would have liked to have capitalised on her discovery immediately. But it wasn't safe, and she'd had to lie low before eventually skipping to the continent with the Infant Phenomenon. At least she knew the act would make her a good living.

Yes, a hall north of the river would have been much better. But the contracts offered had been poor. She suspected that word was spreading that Aurora Scarletti was getting a bit too old to be called the Infant Phenomenon any more. Never mind; Lizzie had another, much more lucrative, use for the brat.

Only Thomas Campion had made a halfway decent offer for the act. At first Lizzie had thought it was too dangerous to accept. It was so close to the Victorious, but fortuitously that had closed down months before so it was less likely that anyone would be around to recognise her from the old days.

She was most wary of Thomas Campion

himself. But he had never known her name, and it had been the most fleeting encounter all those years ago. Besides, she had changed substantially. Her luxurious dark hair was now sparse and grey, and she had put on a considerable amount of weight. She was almost unrecognisable from the wiry woman she had been almost thirteen years before.

Lizzie Gawkin heaved herself huffing and puffing from the hansom cab, which had stopped outside the post office. She had a letter in her hand. The Infant Phenomenon pushed back a ringlet and tried to read the name and address while at the same time appearing to have absolutely no interest in it at all. She couldn't see the addressee but she could see part of the address: Silver Square.

"You wait there, Aurora," ordered Lizzie. "I won't be long."

Lizzie disappeared into the post office. Aurora sighed. She hated trailing around after Lizzie, she hated the scratchy taffeta frocks that Lizzie insisted she wear, and she hated the thought of arriving at a new music hall where she knew that she would prove an instant disappointment. She was way too old to be billed as an Infant Phenomenon. When she had performed as a tot she could hold any audience in the palm of her hand, but as she had grown older, audiences had become a lot less forgiving. But Lizzie wouldn't let her change the act, said it wasn't worth the effort. The last time she had suggested it Lizzie had pinched her until her arms were black and blue.

She'd be lonely at Campion's too. Lizzie insisted that they kept themselves to themselves. Aurora had learned the hard way that there was no point in trying to make friends at the halls; it was easier to be surly and disagreeable from the start rather than suffer the disappointment of having friendship snatched away just as it was blossoming.

"I don't want my treasure mixing with nasty, common hall people," said Lizzie. "Our business is our business. We don't want other people's noses prying into our secrets."

Aurora was increasingly confident that all Lizzie's secrets were nasty ones. She had lost count of the number of times they had unexpectedly moved on from halls before her contract had expired. In Dieppe one evening the drunken owner had chased her and Lizzie off the premises shouting in French that Lizzie was a "blackmailing cow" and that he would call the police if either of them ever set foot in the hall again.

Aurora glanced down at the floor of the cab, where a folded piece of newsprint lay near the door. Lizzie must have dropped it as she'd left the cab. Aurora picked it up and smoothed it out. It was about a toff called Lord Henry Easingford who was about to join the Privy Council. Aurora didn't know what the Privy Council was but it sounded grand. She wondered why Lizzie had been keeping it. But then she wondered a great many things about Lizzie, not least whether Lizzie Gawkin really was her aunt and what had happened to her real mother and father.

Every time she asked, the story changed. She had a hazy memory of dancing in a great black-and-white tiled hall and being chucked under the chin and given a sweet for her performance. A place where you looked through bars when you looked out of the window. She decided to try again to take a peek inside the small, locked lacquered box that Lizzie always kept in the trunk that she stored in the dressing room of any theatre they visited. Lizzie had been drinking more gin recently. If she bided her time, Aurora was sure she'd get a chance to filch the keys. Maybe she would at last find out who her parents were and where she came from.

She leaned out of the window of the cab. London was frightening, noisy and dirty, but it was exciting too. She saw a young tousle-haired man of about thirty walking towards her along the street. His clothes were worn, even slightly ragged, but brightly coloured. He was wearing a Lincoln-green waistcoat and matching cap and he walked with an easy, confident gait. He had an open, handsome face and he smiled generously at people as he passed. Aurora could spot an actor from a mile away and she was confident that this young man was an actor. She wondered if he worked at Campion's. It wasn't far away, just up an alley closer to the river.

As the young man reached the door of the post office, Lizzie emerged, heading straight for the cab. She was pulling on her dogskin gloves and, not looking where she was going, she barged into the young man. She dropped a glove and let out a tirade of foul-mouthed abuse that made Aurora long for the earth to swallow her up. If the man did work at Campion's and recognised them later it would be mortifying. But the young man was unfazed. He gracefully retrieved the dropped glove for Lizzie and presented it to her with the sunniest of smiles while bowing his head ever so politely. Lizzie gave a tiny squawk and there was something about the way she looked at the young man that made Aurora quite certain Lizzie knew him, and was shocked by this chance meeting. But the man had simply smiled again, completely unconcerned, and continued onward in the direction of Campion's, leaving Lizzie staring after him as if she'd seen a ghost.

Lizzie collected her wits and waddled over to the window of the cab. She flung a few coins into Aurora's lap.

"Go back to the lodging house and wait for me there. I've got business that I need to attend to," she said.

She set off in pursuit of the young man. The hansom cab had only gone a few yards when it was held up by a dray cart that had lost a wheel. Aurora poked her head out of the window and looked back. She saw the young man turn down a narrow street towards the river. A few seconds later, Lizzie turned down the street after him.

It was almost noon before Lizzie returned to the lodging house, by which time the city was cocooned in a fog that enveloped it like a yellow shroud. Lizzie was unusually dishevelled and in an even more foul mood than ever. Aurora noticed that she had a speck of blood on one of her dogskin gloves.

6

With her back to the sagging, mould-covered wall, Effie slid down on to the damp earth floor and twisted a strand of her dirty blonde hair around her finger. The one-roomed tenement in Shoreditch that she had called home was open to the world. Even the door had been removed. Effie guessed somebody had wanted it for firewood. The glass had gone from the single squat window too. She felt desolate.

Her stomach was yawning with hunger. She hadn't eaten anything since yesterday. But it was her heart that felt empty. The look of despair in her mother's eyes that morning as the judge pronounced sentence – nine years in Holloway Prison for stealing a pocket watch – was etched on to her memory. Effie had wanted to shout at the judge about how it was their landlord's lackey, Josiah Pinch, who should be in the dock. How he waited for them at the tenement off the Bethnal Green Road, stick in hand, ready to deliver a beating if they ever dared to return empty-handed. How he enjoyed frightening them, half raising his bowler hat at them in a gesture that was not respectful but threatening. How they had tried to leave and make a fresh start in Hackney, but how Josiah Pinch had found them and dragged them back, beating her mother so badly that she hadn't been able to walk for a week. Then he'd stroked the waxed moustache that sat like a slug on his top lip and walked away, whistling his favourite tune, "Pop Goes the Weasel". Effie had opened her mouth to speak but she saw the warning look in her mother's eye, telling her to remain silent and not to draw attention to herself.

Now her mother was behind bars, there was nothing keeping her in Shoreditch. Effie stood up and walked down the street, peering into the dark, smoky tenements squirming with adults, shoeless children and yapping dogs. Most people looked away. They had their own problems; they didn't want trouble knocking at the door. Everyone lived on the edge here.

Only Grace Dorset, who lived further down on the other side of the street, invited Effie close to her smouldering fire. Effie's mum had liked Grace and Ned, said they were kind and not yet worn down by Shoreditch life. Now Grace hugged Effie while she cried for her mother, and gave her some tea and bread that she could ill afford to spare.

Grace didn't judge, not like some people. She told Effie that things might be looking up for them at last – Ned had left very early that morning to go and see Thomas Campion.

"Oh, I really hope he's going to accept Mr Campion's job offer. He got another letter from America this morning, see. From Chicago. He won't say who he writes to there. But he gets letters back, and whoever it is I think it was that person who sent him to visit that Eliza in the workhouse. He seemed very excited by it, and told me everything was going to be all right and he'd explain everything on his return. Said he might have to go north after going to Campion's, but hoped we'd be proud of him for doing the right thing. It was lovely to see him so excited since giving up *King Lear* in Oxford."

"Why'd he do that?" asked Effie.

Grace sighed. "This actor joined the company, got the part of the Fool, see, and said he'd met Ned's double in Chicago when he'd been in a production of *Romeo and Juliet* there. Asked if he might be a relation. Showed him a review cut from a Chicago newspaper. The photograph was blurry, but even I could see the likeness. Ned seemed quite rattled by it. Maybe because the actor in the picture, I can't remember his name, Ed something, was doing really well. He'd even been called the greatest Romeo of his generation and was about to play Hamlet. Ned said he had to go to Yorkshire immediately. I guessed it must be to see someone in his family. When he returned, he said he was leaving *King Lear* and we were moving to London. Just like that. No discussion, which isn't like Ned. We've always decided everything together."

"Doesn't say much about his family, does he?"

Grace sighed. "I can't even say for sure that the man I love really is called Ned Dorset. Once when he was upset he said that he'd taken his name off a gravestone."

Effie pulled a face. "How strange. Do you think it could be true?"

"I don't know," said Grace, shaking her head. "He said afterwards he'd been joking. Maybe he was. But since what happened at Oxford I've thought he seemed frightened, and it was because of something in his past. But maybe things are changing and he'll take up Thomas Campion's offer of a job and we can get back on our feet again." Grace waved a hand. "I know we can do better than this."

Effie nodded. She knew about better. Her mum had always wanted better for her too. They had both tasted better when her mum had worked at the match factory. There had been cosy suppers of meat puddings and saveloys. They had even occasionally gone to the Fortune to see the glamorous and saucy Tilly Tiptree or hear chimney-sweep-turned-music-hall star Sam Harries sing. It made her mum grow bright-eyed and sentimental and tell Effie stories of when she was a young seamstress over in Southwark on the other side of the Thames. Effie hadn't realised it then but although money was tight, they had been richer than the old Queen herself.

Then came the factory accident. Her mother's burned arm had never worked properly after that. She had been laid off. They didn't even pay her the wages they owed, saying the accident had been her own fault. Now her mum could no longer afford for Effie to buy the watercress in winter and lavender in summer that she hawked in the streets for a small profit. They quickly fell behind with the rent. The rent collector had put the frighteners on them, then he had sent round Josiah Pinch, a nasty piece of work, who said that he would help them with the landlord if they helped him out in return.

He set her and her mum to work. Thieving. Effie created a disturbance and acted as lookout; her mum did the prigging. Effie's hazel eyes welled at the memory of her mother's shame and self-hatred. It had been such a short journey from just enough to absolutely nothing, from full stomachs to empty, and from respectability to Holloway Prison.

Grace pressed a tuppence that she couldn't afford into Effie's hand and waved the girl's protests away.

"Maybe the deuce will change your luck, Effie."

Effie hugged Grace. "Good luck to you too, Gracie."

Effie set off towards the river. She would go south to Southwark or Bermondsey. Maybe she could get work as a seamstress. She would begin again. Somewhere Josiah Pinch would never find her. She would rely on nobody but herself, work hard and when her mother was released from the forbidding brick fortress of Holloway Prison, she would have a home for her.

She walked across London Bridge with hundreds of others. In the middle, she stopped and looked back. But the swirling fog obscured everything. She steeled herself and walked onward, knowing that all the love and warmth and laughter she had ever known in the world were behind her.

7

It was one of those bitter nights when chilly fingers of foul-smelling fog crept off the Thames and curled into the narrow, muddy warren of streets where Southwark and Bermondsey collide. As Effie was walking over London Bridge, Rose was centre stage at Campion's. She was playing the doomed young Prince Arthur in a scene from Shakespeare's play *King John*.

On a good night some of the more sentimental members of the audience would be moved to tears by the sight of poor little Arthur facing up to his uncle's wickedness with such pluck. But no night had been good at Campion's recently.

The audience was sparse again and the blonde wig on Rose's head itched and kept sliding over her eyes. Some men with mutton-chop whiskers were propping up the carved mahogany bar at the back of the auditorium and laughing raucously among themselves; a woman in the front was so gripped by the drama that she had fallen fast asleep, her bonnet askew. Her snores were louder than a railway engine.

O'Leary, who was playing the man sent to murder Arthur, put his red, veined face close up to Rose's as he reached the end of his speech. In his prime, O'Leary had been a fine actor and an even better balladeer. But drink and age had taken their toll. He should have retired from the stage years ago, but kind-hearted Thomas knew that if he did, O'Leary would drink himself to death within months. He needed the camaraderie of Campion's to stay alive.

On stage, O'Leary tried and failed to suppress a belch. Rose tried and failed not to wince. The fumes suggested that he had already enjoyed an early supper of bloaters and beer. Rose sighed, and her mind wandered. Campion's was hardly the Theatre Royal, the Haymarket or the Lyceum, which was run by the great actor-manager Henry Irving and where she'd seen the incomparable Ellen Terry play Cordelia in *King Lear*. But it was home.

With luck, it would be busier later in the evening. The crowd would be rowdier and sated with beer and stewed oysters. Then the bill would feature saucy comic songs, daredevil acrobats, murder scenes from the melodramas, ballet dancers showing their ankles, and Belle Canterbury, daringly dressed in a sailor suit, looking wistfully up to the gallery and singing her signature song about how her heart had been broken by a faithless lover.

Rose tried to get back into character, but she was distracted by all the shouting coming from the stage door. She suddenly sensed movement up in the gallery too, which was closed due to lack of custom. She risked a quick glance upwards past the twisted gilt-painted pillars that seemed far too fragile to support the horseshoe-shaped gallery. That was when she spotted Ned. He was leaning over the ledge and watching her intently with a big, wide boyish grin. There was something odd, almost insubstantial and ghost-like about him. She wondered if there was something wrong with her eyes.

Rose carried on with the scene, despite the distraction of Ned and the increasing commotion from backstage. She blinked into the semi-darkness and sneaked another look at Ned. His smile had gone, to be replaced by a much more serious and urgent demeanour. He seemed to be trying to tell her something. He was miming holding a baby and he kept pointing at her and then pointing at the baby and mouthing words she couldn't make out. She wondered if he was trying to tell her that he and Grace were having another baby. But why wouldn't he just pop backstage after the show and tell her? She was pleased to see him, anyway, hoping it meant that he had come to accept Thomas's offer of a job.

The Shakespeare scene was drawing to an end. It was just as well. The small audience was becoming restive. There were even a few catcalls. Rose glanced up again to the gallery. Ned had gone. She was surprised. She hadn't noticed him leave. She was disappointed too. Her acting was clearly so bad that even he, who had always been her biggest fan, couldn't be bothered to stay and watch the end of the scene. She suddenly felt less keen to see him again.

After the desultory applause, she walked gloomily into the wings, tugged off her wig and britches, and pulled on the skirt she had left by the side of the stage. Such mayhem had broken out by the stage door that all thought of Ned went straight out of her mind. Trunks and boxes were piled high, and a very large woman who looked as if she had been stuffed like a sausage into a tartan dress was waving her arms theatrically and fanning her crimson face.

"Sorry, missus," said one of the stagehands. "The gaffer – I mean Mr Campion – 'ad to go out. He should be back soon."

"It's an outrage!" screeched the red-faced woman. "Mr Campion promised he'd be here to greet the arrival of his new star in person."

Rose stared. She had never seen a grown woman stamp her foot before. It was hard to resist the urge to laugh. Next to the red-faced woman stood a slight, scowling girl around Rose's age with rusty brown hair twisted into ringlets. Dressed in wine-coloured taffeta, the girl wore six matching ribbons in her hair.

"My precious Aurora, my treasure, is going to be number one on the bill, you know!" continued the woman. "I've never been so insulted!"

She pulled out a silk handkerchief and dabbed at her eyes with it theatrically.

Rose's natural friendliness won out over her

urge to slap the silly woman and tell her to stop making such a fuss.

"Hello," she said cheerfully. "Can I help you?"

The woman in the tartan dress suddenly quietened. She raised a lorgnette to one eye and appraised Rose.

"I should hope so," she said. "I'm Lizzie Gawkin and this is Miss Aurora Scarletti, otherwise known as the amazing Infant Phenomenon. And who might you be?"

"I know who she is," interrupted the girl rudely from under her long dark lashes. "I asked one of the stagehands. He told me all about her, how she was found abandoned on the doorstep and Thomas Campion took her in. She's Rose Campion and I've been watching her act."

The girl looked down her nose at Rose and said the word "act" as if it had a nasty smell. Then she pointedly turned her back. Lizzie raised her lorgnette again and considered Rose with intense interest.

Rose had to suppress an urge to laugh at the girl's rudeness. But the name "Infant Phenomenon" sparked a memory. She'd heard about the child-star and her battleaxe aunt from a troupe of castanet dancers who had passed briefly through Campion's over a year ago and had seen the Infant Phenomenon perform in a hall near Paris. One of the girls in the troupe had done a very funny impression of the act. She tied her hair in bunches, put a finger in her mouth and lisped a popular song as if she was five years old, and then ran around the room pirouetting and curtseying like a prize pony tossing its mane.

"It was probably really charming and raked in the money when she was seven or eight," she'd said, "but the bairn's growing up fast. She's in long skirts. It's a shame cos she's got talent. If only her aunt would let her grow up and do summat new."

Rose knew that things must be desperate for Thomas to even think of bringing the Infant Phenomenon to Campion's. It was the kind of simpering act he hated.

"I demand to see Mr Campion immediately!" screeched Lizzie Gawkin. "I will not allow my little treasure to be insulted like this."

Rose stole another glance at the girl's sulky face. She was staring at her aunt in a way that was hard to interpret. Then she caught Rose looking at her and gave a tight little smile.

"Don't worry, Rose Campion," she said in the kind of careful English that comes from spending a long time abroad. "You don't have to embarrass yourself on stage any longer. I'll be playing Arthur from now on. And all the other child roles too. It's written into my contract."

Rose was stunned. She must be lying. Thomas would never allow it! He knew how much these small opportunities to act meant to her.

At that moment Thomas walked through the door. "Mrs Gawkin, my apologies. I was delayed on business. Welcome to Campion's."

He took her gloved hand, and raised it gallantly to his lips. For just a second Rose saw a puzzled look on his face as if he was trying to remember where he'd seen the woman before.

"Mr Campion, pleased, I'm sure," said Lizzie with all the affectation of a duchess. "This is my little treasure, Aurora, the Infant Phenomenon."

Thomas and the girl bowed and bobbed. Rose could see him trying to disguise his disbelief; she was prepared to bet that Lizzie hadn't been completely truthful about the "infant's" age. She was almost as tall as Rose.

"Mrs Gawkin, will you honour me by joining me in a glass of brandy or port?" asked Thomas.

"I'd be delighted, Mr Campion," said Lizzie. "Just to get over the shock of arriving and not getting the appropriate welcome. By the way, Mr Campion, before I forget – I am expecting a very important letter. Please ensure that it gets to me safely."

Thomas nodded and turned to Rose. Before he could say anything, she opened her mouth to speak.

"Thomas," she said, a chill in her voice, "is it true that Miss Scarletti will be playing all the child roles from now on?"

Thomas went to put his hand on Rose's shoulder but she pulled away. She knew he would only have brought the Infant Phenomenon to Campion's if he thought the act was going to help save the music hall, and she had vowed that she would do all she could to help too. But she had never imagined it would mean giving up performing the roles she loved to someone else. Her world had shifted; the future was uncertain and she suddenly felt dreadfully insecure.

"Rose," said Thomas, and she could hear the desperation in his voice. "I was going to tell you.

Tonight. I promise. I got my dates mixed up and I thought they were arriving tomorrow. Let's talk about it later. There's plenty of other things for you to do to help Campion's. We really need you."

Rose could see Lizzie Gawkin clocking the tension between her and Thomas and filing it away in her head for future use. She didn't want to give the woman the satisfaction of knowing how angry she was, but she couldn't help herself. She felt so hurt by Thomas's failure to warn her, and by the other girl's rudeness about her acting. Maybe she was right. Maybe Rose had no talent and Thomas had only been humouring her because he thought of her like a daughter.

"That's fine, Thomas," she said coolly. "Let me know when you've got a spare five minutes and we can talk about my new duties."

Rose turned on her heel and walked out of the stage door but not before she had seen the look of hurt on Thomas's face.

8

Rose marched down Hangman's Alley towards the river. Somebody was standing in the shadows near the end of the alley, whistling "Pop Goes the Weasel". It sounded eerie in the fog that was filling up her lungs like treacle. She crossed the slippery riverside path and scrambled on to the wall, sitting there in the chill exhausted by hurt and anxiety.

Below her, the ghostly figures of the mudlarks could just be made out in the fog as they scavenged on the exposed shoreline. Rose watched as a small grubby boy who looked about seven sifted through the oozing black sludge, searching for metal and bones. His fingers were bleeding.

"No luck?" called Rose. Only yesterday she

had bought an old bicycle off the mudlarks, a strange, misshapen metal fish that they had rescued from the river. Rose was sure that she and the stagehands could do it up; she wondered whether they might even be able to incorporate it in an act.

The boy shook his head. "Naught but red worms. All fat and bloated on the body they fished out the river down by London Bridge at noon," he said.

"Man or woman?" asked Rose.

"Man, poor soul," said the boy. "By the look of 'im, they say he can only have just gone in. Eels 'adn't 'ad time to get 'is eyes."

Rose shivered, felt in her pocket and found a farthing.

"Here," she called to the boy and she tossed him the coin. He rewarded her with a broad, toothy grin and went back to his sieving. It made her think how much better her life was than that of the mudlarks. Even if she could no longer act, she still had plenty of food to eat and somewhere warm to sleep.

She suddenly felt ashamed of the way she had treated Thomas, who she knew loved her like a daughter. He was so worried all the time about losing Campion's, it was hardly surprising that he had mixed up the date of the arrival of the Infant Phenomenon. Rose just hoped Aurora would bring in the crowds.

"Come and find me at Campion's if you dredge up anything good," she shouted to the boy. Then she slipped off the wall and started to make her way back to find Thomas and make things up with him. Rose never bore a grudge for long, and neither did Thomas. She suddenly realised how hungry she was and stopped to buy a pie. She was about to bite through the crust into the steaming gravy when a commotion started up in the street. A boy with a livid scar down his face tore across the road followed by a girl around Rose's age. She was as thin as paper and she had lanky blonde hair, a heart-shaped face and fierce hazel eyes. She was shouting indignantly after the boy.

"Give it back!" she cried. "Give me back me money, you thief."

The boy didn't stop, and disappeared down a muddy, rutted lane that led into a maze of streets, then vanished into the fog. The girl, still shouting, went to follow him but Rose caught her arm.

"Let it go. He's one of the Tanner Street boys, and you don't mess with them any more than you mess with a pit bull terrier. I wouldn't go down there, if I were you. Anyone you meet will as soon as cut your throat and steal the clothes off your back as give you the time of day."

The girl shook off her arm.

"He tricked me. Told me he'd take me to a lodging house and get me a place on a rag-gathering gang if I gave him me deuce." The girl's hazel eyes welled with furious tears. She was shaking her head at her own stupidity. "He's a low-down, lying prigger."

A man in the crowd, which had gathered to watch the unfolding drama, jeered.

"And you're the Queen of Sheba. More like a little pickpocket yourself."

The girl raised her fists. "I ain't no pickpocket," she said indignantly. "Honest as the day, that's me."

The man laughed at her fierceness and Rose laid a soothing hand on her shoulder.

"Here," said Rose, offering her untouched pie. "Have this."

The girl eyed it for a moment and then took the pie, stuffed it ravenously into her mouth and chewed furiously. Gravy ran down her chin.

"I ain't no pickpocket," she insisted again through a mouthful of food.

"Are you all on your own? No family?" asked Rose.

The girl shook her head.

"Do you have somewhere to go for the night?" Rose continued.

The girl stuck out her chin defiantly and frowned. She wasn't going to let this one trick her like the scar-faced boy had. She wouldn't trust her too easily.

"You think I was born yesterday," she said hotly. "I ain't no pigeon. I know how to look after meself."

"Pleased to hear it," said Rose. "But if you ever need help, come to Campion's."

The girl put her head on one side like an inquisitive bird. Campion's! Grace Dorset had been talking about it only this afternoon. Maybe it was fate?

"Campion's Palace of Varieties and Wonders," said Rose proudly, by way of explanation. "It's not far. Down Hangman's Alley."

"The music hall," breathed the girl, and her eyes filled with sunshine at the thought.

"We put on melodramas and pantomimes too." Rose smiled encouragingly.

A struggle was taking place in the girl's face. She looked back down the dark lane where the boy had disappeared. She'd like to try to get her deuce back, prove to herself and this girl that she wasn't an easy mark. Go to Campion's with her stomach full and her head held high.

"Mebbe I'll come by later," she said hesitantly.

"Suit yourself," said Rose. "You'd be welcome. Any time. Ask for Rose."

The girl bit her lip and nodded. "I'm Effie."

Rose reached into her pocket and handed Effie a penny. The girl protested, but Rose wouldn't take no for an answer.

Effie watched Rose disappear into the fog. Every bone in her body was telling her to run after her. She had felt safe with Rose. She looked down at the penny in her palm. Maybe it would change her luck. She could always go to Campion's tomorrow or the day after if need be. It would be her safety net, and she felt better just knowing it was there. But she desperately wanted to stand on her own two feet, prove to herself, her mum and the world that she could do it.

9

Aurora sat, bored, at a table in the Four Cripples, just round the corner from Campion's, trying to pretend she was listening to Lizzie's rambling monologue. Thomas Campion had been insistent that, since he had not been expecting the Infant Phenomenon and Lizzie until the next day, she must rest tonight. Aurora rather doubted that Thomas's idea of her resting was sitting in the Four Cripples watching Lizzie drink gin. The woman had been drinking steadily for the last two hours. It was making her garrulous. She kept leaning forward and breathing gin fumes into Aurora's face, making the girl recoil in disgust.

"Auntie," said Aurora tentatively, "I was thinking about trying out something new in the act…"

Lizzie eyed her sharply and took another slurp of gin.

"Don't get any ideas about setting up on your own, girl," she said. "It's a cruel world out there. Without me to look out for you, you'd be no better than a beggar on the street. Don't start believing all that nonsense I put out about you being a treasure. Without me, you're nothing." She lurched drunkenly across the table and spoke in a conspiratorial whisper. "Mind, I do have some real treasure, oh yes, and you'll find out about that soon enough." She knocked back more gin. Her eyes looked distant. "It's not just silver and gold that's precious. There's something that's worth far more: knowledge and information. I'm just biding my time and then Lizzie Gawkin will be richer than the Queen of England." She slumped forward again and, resting her cheek on the table, her eyelids flickered and she began snoring quietly.

Aurora looked away in disgust. The man at the next table in the low-crowned bowler hat drank the last of his ale, dabbed his slug-like moustache with a handkerchief and left.

She looked around the grimy public house

and sighed. For a moment she was tempted just to stand up and walk out of the Four Cripples, walk out on Lizzie and walk out of the life she was leading. But where would she go? What would she do to survive? Lizzie was right, it was a cruel world out there, and she had no doubt that Lizzie would hunt her down. And Aurora knew that with Lizzie's foul temper the consequences of that for her would be very bad indeed. Without family or friends, she was trapped. She might just as well be behind bars.

She supposed she would have to wake Lizzie up and help her back to Campion's. She heaved the woman up, and Lizzie fell heavily back in her chair with her mouth open, a trail of dribble on her chin. Aurora shook Lizzie's shoulder to make her stand and they tottered towards Campion's with Lizzie leaning heavily on the girl.

As they entered the yard Aurora saw Thomas give Rose a quick hug and disappear back inside the theatre. Clearly the two of them had made up. Aurora felt a stab of terrible loneliness. Even though she knew that Thomas was not Rose's real father, he behaved like one. Aurora wished she knew her own father.

Rose turned a cartwheel. One of the ballet dancers shouted something to her and Rose threw back her head and roared with laughter. Her eyes shone like stars. She looked up, spied Aurora and immediately rushed over to help her. Aurora felt terrible, regretting all the terrible things that she had said to Rose on her arrival. If she had just kept her mouth shut maybe Rose might have become her friend. She needed one more than ever. She was about to apologise to Rose and try to start again when Lizzie jerked awake and began waving her arms around alarmingly and cussing. She and Rose heaved her towards the stage door.

"A letter's come for you by the evening post, Lizzie Gawkin," said O'Leary, manning the stage door as usual. He pushed it into her hand and she thrust it clumsily in her pocket. By the open gate of the yard, a moustachioed man in a bowler turned and sauntered away, whistling "Pop Goes the Weasel" as he went.

10

Rose watched from the side of the stage as Belle Canterbury finished her signature song. Belle's voice rose hauntingly and with a purity that sent a shiver down Rose's spine.

It was a week since Aurora and Lizzie had arrived and the hall was packed. It was warm with the fug of pale ale, gin, shrimps, oysters and the gaslights, and the good cheer of an audience who were delighted to forget about the daily grind of their lives for a few brief hours and be transported to another world. Rose loved Campion's when it was like this; it felt like something out of a fairy tale wrapped in its own secret golden web of magic. The gilt mirrors glittered against the eggshell-blue walls. The chandelier shivered and sparkled. Everyone in the audience suddenly looked beautiful; even the most ragged and patched glowed as if lit from within.

She glanced at the faces of the audience, who were all on their feet and demanding a encore so that they could sing along. Men, women and even some children were gazing at the boyish Belle longingly as if she was the most romantic thing they had ever seen.

Rose grinned to herself. Little did they know that away from the haze of the limelight, and without her rouged lips and cheeks, smoky eyes and the sailor suit that gave her such boyish appeal, Belle was a plain, shy young woman who lived quietly with her invalid mother in Lant Street. Her real name was Prudence Smith. But Prudence had the voice of a nightingale and when she stepped on to the stage she was transformed into something wistful and unworldly. On stage she was endlessly fascinating, but in her everyday skirts nobody looked at her twice. The young men who hung around the stage door after her act, hoping to thrust flowers into her hand or take her to supper, never realised that the homely young woman with glasses and a long plait slipping quietly by them was none other than the glamorously crop-haired and alluring Belle Canterbury. She had had plenty of offers to work in other halls, including far grander ones across the river, but Belle refused them all. Campion's suited her. It was near her mum, to whom she was devoted, and Thomas was always understanding when the old lady took a turn for the worse and Belle needed time away from the hall.

The crowd fell silent as Belle began to sing again, and Gus, the stage manager, nodded at Rose, who slipped along the corridor to warn the ballet girls that their number was imminent. She met Thomas along the way. He was looking more cheerful than he had for ages, and once again she felt guilty that she'd thrown a strop over the Infant Phenomenon act. She knew he had to do anything necessary to save the music hall they both loved.

"Ah, Rosie," he said. "I've been looking for you. I've had a note from Grace Dorset. She's worried about Ned. Apparently he set off this way a week ago and never returned. She's beside herself with worry, and little Freddie is in the fever hospital so she can't come looking herself.

You haven't by any chance seen him at all since the day of our little tea party last month?"

"Yes," said Rose, looking puzzled. "I did see him. He was up in the gallery, watching me and O'Leary doing the scene from *King John*. I assumed he'd come to see you about the job and slipped in to see the first show. But then with all the mayhem surrounding Aurora and Lizzie's arrival I quite forgot about seeing him."

"So you're sure it was the same day that Lizzie and Aurora arrived?"

Rose nodded.

"And you didn't speak to him?"

"I didn't get the chance," said Rose. "One minute he was in the gallery watching me, and the next he had just completely disappeared. Like a ghost." She paused and frowned. "But I got the impression he was trying to tell me something. He was miming holding a baby and pointing at me. But I haven't a clue what he was trying to say."

Thomas looked anxious. "I'd better let Grace know he's been here. But it won't set her mind at rest." He sighed. "It doesn't set mine at rest either. Ned's a reliable boy, and he'd never stay away from Grace and Freddie for long without very good reason. I hope nothing bad has happened."

From the auditorium came the sound of the crowd shouting and laughing.

"Just listen to them roar," said Thomas.

"Almost a full house," replied Rose. "Lots of big-spending swells in too."

"Lots of clearing up after," said Thomas, "but plenty of money in everyone's pockets."

Then they both smiled and said in unison: "Every crowd has a silver lining."

Rose had to admit Aurora *was* bringing in the crowds. She hated the way Lizzie Gawkin lorded it over everyone, and the way Campion's now resounded to the sound of her high, thin voice bleating in perpetual complaint. She particularly hated the way that Lizzie kept looking at her, as if the woman knew something about her that Rose didn't know herself.

"It's rude to stare," Rose told her one day.

Lizzie had squawked with laughter. "Well, you would know all about being rude, because you're such a la-di-da lady, aren't you?"

It was only for Thomas's sake that Rose had bitten her tongue. Still, she had to admit that though Aurora was hardly an infant and nowhere close to being a phenomenon, she really was a very good actress. She had a good line in satirical songs. The crowd loved it when she dressed up as a shy debutante being taken to the zoo by her fiancé and fainting at the sight of every wild animal. They enjoyed it when she danced, and did duologues snitched from popular melodramas, the bloodier and more murderous the better.

Jem Dorries was often roped in to perform opposite her. With his good looks, Jem was a favourite with the ladies. None of them realised that the multi-talented Jem was also the turbaned sword-swallower and juggler, Ali the Great Wizard of the Orient. At Campion's, everyone was a master of disguise.

Rose knocked on the door of the ballet girls' dressing room. Since the arrival of Aurora and her aunt, the ballet girls had been forced to share with all the other female artistes, and though there had been mutterings of discontent at the star treatment for the newcomers, they had all cheerfully mucked in together with much laughter. Even the shy Belle had gone in with the other girls and enjoyed their gentle teasing, ribald jokes and singalongs.

Much to Lizzie's fury, who demanded it must be located immediately, the key to the small dressing room couldn't be found anywhere. Her rage increased when the ballet girls kept drifting back into their former dressing room, on endless quests to find lost stockings, garters and hatpins, forgotten love letters from admirers and, in the case of Lottie, the two white mice that she kept in a cage under a table behind a heap of discarded costumes.

Lizzie had screeched loudly when Lottie emerged from under the table, triumphantly holding the cage aloft. But everyone else agreed with Rose when she said that it was the white mice who should be outraged at having to share a dressing room with Lizzie. She blurted the words out backstage before realising Aurora was standing nearby. Rose blushed, but for a second she thought she saw a gleam of amusement in Aurora's green eyes.

Rose poked her head into the dressing room where the ballet girls were getting ready to let them know their cue would be soon. It smelled of rose water, sweat, powder, rouge and the burned cork many of the girls used to darken their lashes and outline their eyes. Some of the girls were trying to run through the routine in the cramped space.

"Hello, Rosie. How are you?" asked Lottie, and several of the girls immediately broke into a chorus of "Rosie, Rosie, give me your answer, do, I'm half crazy…"

Rose grinned. "Five minutes and you're on. You need to come now or there'll be trouble."

"Lor, I'm nowhere near ready. Be a duck, Rosie," said Lottie, "an' pop into their royal highnesses' dressing room next door and get me headdress. I know I left it there. It'll be on the window ledge."

Rose nodded, and walked back down the corridor. The door to the dressing room was ajar so she peeped through the crack. The room appeared to be empty so she pushed the open door and walked in, then immediately realised her mistake. Lizzie was sitting on the floor half hidden behind the open lid of a large trunk. In her shock at Rose's intrusion, the woman leapt to her feet, holding a lacquered box in her hand. Rose spied a flash of silver, a blue ribbon and some papers before Lizzie snapped the box lid shut. She staggered heavily towards Rose, her face contorted in fury. Rose could smell gin fumes.

"You little spy!" she screeched. "Who sent you to pry into my affairs?"

"Nobody," stuttered Rose. "I wasn't snooping. I just came for Lottie's headdress." She pointed towards the window ledge where it sat, rather crumpled, exactly where Lottie said it would be. "She needs it for the cancan. I'm sorry, I thought the dressing room was empty or I'd have knocked."

Lizzie narrowed her eyes, but seemed a little mollified.

"Take it," she said with a nod towards the window ledge. Rose picked the headdress up and went to leave.

"What did you see?" demanded Lizzie sharply.

"I didn't see anything, honest," said Rose, opening her eyes very wide like the most innocent of cherubs. Then, although she knew she really shouldn't, she just couldn't resist adding, "Apart from the dead body, of course."

Lizzie turned white with shock and then ugly red blotches of fury bloomed on her cheeks.

"Only joking," said Rose hastily, backing towards the door and bumping into Aurora.

The girl was taking her jacket off as she came into the room and Rose couldn't help notice that her arms were covered in bruises, as if somebody had been pinching her hard. Aurora saw Rose looking and pulled her jacket back on quickly, but at that moment Lottie put her head around the door.

"Come on, Rosie! Move yourself. I need that headdress now or I'm going to miss my cue."

Rose followed Lottie down the corridor, all the while wondering what it was that Lizzie was so keen to hide from prying eyes.

11

Effie stood shivering outside Campion's and watched as the crowds pushed their way into the music hall. There was a hint of snow in the air. She could hear music and laughter coming from inside, and the frosted windows gave off an enticing golden glow.

Effie blew on her hands. She longed to go in and be enveloped by the warmth and see the wonders inside for herself. But she didn't have the money. For the past ten days she had just about kept body and soul together. But every second had felt like a struggle. She'd had some luck, mind. Running errands for one of the coffee-stall keepers had kept her in hot drinks and bread; she got two days' work at one of the laundries amid the steaming coppers. But the last couple of days it had turned colder and her luck had run out too. There had been no work at the laundry and the coffee-stall keeper had been replaced by his less-friendly brother.

That morning she had stood in a crowd next to a well-dressed woman whose purse was poking out of her open bag. The temptation to dip her hand in and prig it was almost overwhelming. But the image of her mother looking at her sorrowfully from the dock of the Old Bailey popped into her head and she hesitated. At that moment the woman looked down, realised her bag was open and pulled the strings tight shut. Then she'd glanced at Effie suspiciously and moved away. It made Effie feel guilty even though she'd done nothing.

Now as she loitered outside Campion's in a mean drizzle of rain she wished she had taken the purse. She wondered about going into the yard and asking for Rose. But Rose had probably forgotten all about her by now. The door to Campion's opened and there was a gust of warmth as a group came out, their eyes shining and their cheeks glowing. They were muffled against the cold and they didn't even notice Effie as they walked down the road. She was just one of thousands of ragged children who thronged the London streets.

Two carriages loomed out of the swirling fog and pulled up outside the music hall. A group of toffs got out, laughing loudly. They had some young women with them. Their clothes were bright in the glimmer of the street lamps and Effie thought they looked like beautiful butterflies against the inky darkness of the street. The group thronged towards the entrance that was giving out a light like molten honey.

"I say!" said one of the men loudly. "This is slumming it a bit, what!"

"Champagne tastes the same wherever you are," brayed another. "We've come to see the Infant Phenomenon. Let's hope the Infant Phenomenon is ready to see us."

There were cackles.

"I've been before. It's a quaint little down-at-heel place," said another man. "Feels authentic. They're got a good singer too, Belle Canterbury. Wonderful voice. Let's give it a chance. We can always move on to the Alhambra or the Britannia later."

They brushed by Effie without seeing her, even though one of them managed to step heavily on her foot. They flung the door open and swaggered in. Effie peered yearningly into the melting light. She took a step towards it. The music and laughter clawed at her heart as she remembered being at the Fortune with her mum. She took another step forward.

The group were by the table where the box office was set up, jostling impatiently. Unseen, Effie wormed her way into the centre of the crowd, and as the toffs were waved through after paying she slipped in with them. The swells made straight for the mahogany bar. Effie heard them calling loudly for champagne as they were shown towards a table.

Effie looked around quickly and then quietly headed for the gallery. She filled her lungs with the warm mustiness of the place. She picked her way along a bench near the front of the gallery where there was a space next to a large, bad-tempered woman wearing an ugly tartan dress with a lorgnette held to her eyes. She slid into the empty spot. The woman glared at Effie and shuffled slightly to her left. Effie blushed. She was certain the woman thought she was riddled with fleas.

She glanced around her and froze. Sitting right behind the woman was the scar-faced Tanner Street boy who had tricked her out of her money. He hadn't noticed her because he was laughing and joking with his friends. Sitting next to him were three girls who looked as if they could be his sisters. The one right behind Effie was bouncing a gurgling infant on her knee. The child was wearing a grimy bonnet and a handkerchief around her neck.

Effie longed to confront the boy but she knew she'd be a fool to even try. The entire gallery would laugh at her. Instead, she tried to concentrate on the stage where Ali the Great Wizard of the Orient was delighting the crowd by juggling several swords. The man on Effie's other side was handed a steaming pie by his wife. Effie sniffed the delicious aroma and tried not to think of her rumbling stomach. Ali finished his act with a daring display of sword-swallowing and left the stage to enthusiastic applause and much whooping.

A voice came from the wings. "Ladies and gentlemen, I give you Miss Aurora Scarletti, the Infant Phenomenon..."

There was a clash of cymbals that sounded like thunder, a cascade of piano keys and the Infant Phenomenon pranced on to the stage. The audience leaned forward as one, with the large woman in the tartan dress leading the applause.

The girl on the stage began a comic song about a posh girl who goes for a walk across London and repeatedly slips and falls in the mud. The crowd were lapping it up. Effie leaned further forward to watch. The song was reaching its climax where the girl falls in a pile of steaming horse dung. The woman in the tartan dress next to her was screeching encouragement, unaware that the Tanner Street gang were mocking her behind her back.

Effie glanced around the eggshell-blue interior and marvelled at the gilt mirrors. She hugged herself with pleasure. Campion's was so lovely. She caught a glimpse of Rose standing at the entrance to the gallery, watching the stage. Suddenly Rose turned and looked at Effie and grinned at her.

Effie smiled shyly back. Her heart gave a little skip. She had been wrong, Rose did remember her after all! When the Infant

Phenomenon had finished, she would try and talk to Rose. Perhaps Rose would repeat her offer to let Effie spend a few days at Campion's. But of course she wouldn't! If Rose thought Effie could afford to get into the music hall, she'd assume she didn't need help any more. Effie felt tears prick her eyes. She could hardly admit that she had crept into Campion's without paying. It was as good as thieving from Rose. She stole another glance in Rose's direction, but Rose's eyes were fixed on the row behind her. She seemed very interested in the Tanner Street crew and the baby.

The Infant Phenomenon was dancing now. The audience quickly became restive. Effie could see that the girl on the stage had sensed their rowdiness, and she faltered. It only made the crowd noisier. There were some catcalls coming from the gallery and one of the braying toffs from downstairs was baiting her. The woman in tartan was gesturing at the Infant Phenomenon and yelling instructions at her. Effie suddenly felt sorry for her.

The girl glanced up at the balcony and seemed to recover herself. Her mouth was set in a line of determination as she broke into a new comic song. The boisterous crowd quickly quietened and the catcalls died away. They wanted to laugh, and Aurora was now giving them what they wanted.

The woman in the tartan dress lowered herself heavily back on to the bench and as she did so, Effie noticed that her silk handkerchief and her purse were clearly visible, just peeping from inside her pocket. She stared at them both, mesmerised. They were so close. The silk handkerchief alone would be worth at least a shilling. When she and her mum were prigging for Josiah he always said a silk hankie was a better bet than a purse. Easy to steal, easy to sell, and a purse might turn out to be empty.

Suddenly the baby in the row behind started bawling loudly. Effie turned round, and so did everyone else in the vicinity. The woman in tartan craned her neck and shouted, "Stop that racket! Nobody can hear the poor girl sing."

When the woman turned back towards the stage, her purse and handkerchief had vanished, and so had the Tanner Street boys. Effie saw their backs sliding out of the door. She looked around, panicked. Should she raise the alarm? But she couldn't be sure that they had taken the purse. The girls were still sitting on the bench behind, chatting and laughing with a blasé insolence. They didn't look in the slightest bit guilty. The restless anxiety in Effie's manner alerted the woman, who suddenly looked at her sharply. She then looked down at her pocket and patted it frantically.

"I've been robbed!" she screeched, standing up.

Lizzie's voice felt like needles stabbing into Effie's flesh. Effie looked wildly around. She saw Rose move towards her, a troubled look in her eyes.

"My purse, my hankie! Call the rozzers!" cried Lizzie, her voice rising in hysteria.

"It must have been her," said the girls behind, pointing at Effie. "The muck snipe has mizzled that lady's purse and wipe. She deserves the noose."

One of them giggled as if she was looking forward to the spectacle of Effie being hanged by the neck until she was dead. Nobody in the gallery was watching the stage now; all eyes were fixed on Effie and Lizzie, and there was an ugly mood in the air.

A worried-looking Thomas Campion

appeared at the gallery door, eager to calm the situation and protect his music hall's good name. He didn't want the police involved if it could be avoided.

"Make her turn out her pockets!" yelled Lizzie, glowering over Effie like a wild bear.

"Please," whispered Effie, who felt as if her stomach had gone into free fall. "I didn't steal nothing. Cross me heart." She half rose to her feet but as she stood, a handkerchief slithered to the floor. Effie's face was a picture of confusion. Rose snatched the handkerchief up and examined it. She narrowed her eyes at the Tanner Street girls.

"There! Proof!" cried Lizzie triumphantly, without even glancing at the handkerchief.

"I ... I ... I didn't..." stuttered Effie.

"I think you did, my girl," said the girl holding the baby, and she stood up with a swagger.

"Come on, Elsie, Rubes. We ain't going to hang about in a den of tea leaves and cutpurses. It don't become us." The girls swanned towards the door like affronted duchesses. Rose went to open her mouth, but Thomas frowned at her and shook his head. Then he clapped his hands to get the entertainment back underway and the orchestra struck up once more.

He herded Lizzie, Effie and Rose out of the gallery and on to the stairs. Effie was shaking uncontrollably.

"Keep an eye on that one," said Lizzie, "or she'll make a bolt for it, the nasty little dipper. She's a thief; the handkerchief proves it."

"No, it doesn't," said Rose firmly. She was holding the hankie behind her back.

Thomas looked at her quizzically. "What do you mean, Rosie? Spit it out."

"Is this your handkerchief?" Rose asked Lizzie, holding up the handkerchief with a flourish like a magician.

"Of course it's mine!" snapped Lizzie furiously without even deigning to glance at it.

"Oh," said Rose, "and I always had you down as a proper lady."

Lizzie bristled. "I *am* a lady, born and bred; fallen on hard times," she said indignantly.

Rose saw Thomas's mouth twitch.

"Of course," said Rose sympathetically. Then she added, "And as a lady you'd only ever carry a silk hankie…"

Lizzie nodded vigorously. "Of course!"

"So," said Rose, waving the handkerchief in

front of Lizzie, "you'd never use a poor grimy thing like this."

Lizzie took out her lorgnette and peered more closely at the grimy hankie. She saw the poor-quality material and the ungainly stitching.

"That's not my handkerchief. I wouldn't touch such a nasty thing," she said, drawing herself up to her full height.

"I thought so," said Rose. She turned to Effie. "I hate to ask this, but would you mind turning out your pockets, Effie?"

Effie did as she was told. They were empty.

"See?" said Rose. "There's no purse and no silk handkerchief. If this grimy bit of cloth is the only evidence you have of Effie's guilt, then surely we must agree she is entirely innocent of the crime of which you have accused her?"

"Oh, Rosie," said Thomas admiringly. "You're better than a lawyer. Maybe you learned something at that posh school after all." He turned to Lizzie. "Mrs Gawkin?"

Lizzie's face was a mix of the sheepish and the belligerent.

"I still wouldn't trust that guttersnipe," she said, pointing her finger at Effie. She drew herself up. "Besides, I've still suffered a great loss, Mr Campion," she said slyly.

Thomas put an arm around her and guided her down the stairs.

"I'm sure that we can make good your loss, Mrs Gawkin. Will you join me in a glass of brandy and we'll settle it amicably?"

"That's kind of you, Mr Campion," simpered Lizzie. "I will take a small brandy. Only for the shock, of course."

Rose watched them to the bottom of the stairs. Then she turned back to Effie, and in Lizzie's voice she said, "Will you join me in a pie? Only for the shock, of course."

Effie giggled, but her hands were still shaking. "How did you work it out?" she asked shyly.

"Simple. It was the baby," said Rose. "I always try and keep an eye on the Tanner Street lot when they're in. They're trouble, but we can't ban them. They'd put a match to the place. I noticed the babe had a 'kerchief round her neck one minute, and then she didn't. The girls made the baby cry to create a disturbance, the boys prigged the purse and Lizzie's silk handkerchief, and slipped away. Then the girls stayed to create a diversion and peach you up if needed so their brothers would have plenty of time to get away without being fingered."

She took Effie's hand. "Come on," she said. "Let's get those pies."

12

Two days later Effie stood outside Thomas Campion's office with her ear pressed to the door. Her future was at stake.

"Lizzie Gawkin won't have it, Rosie," said Thomas.

"Well, I won't have it any other way," replied Rose hotly. "Effie's staying at Campion's. She's got nowhere else to go, and we can use her. She's a good little grafter. Good with her fingers. Helpful too. She's been painting that bicycle I bought off the mudlarks and mended. Doing it beautifully too."

"We know nothing about Effie. For all we know, she really is a pickpocket. However much you'd like to, Rose, you can't rescue all of London's urchins," said Thomas.

Rose raised her eyebrows in mock horror. "Thomas! Talk about the pot calling the kettle black. So what do you suggest? Sling her back out on the streets like an unwanted kitten? Why don't we just have done with it and drown her in the water barrel?"

"I don't want to put her out," said Thomas, "and in normal circumstances I wouldn't dream of it, but Lizzie Gawkin is insistent that she won't stay another day if Effie is here. She's still convinced that she's a pickpocket, despite the evidence to the contrary. You humiliated her, Rose. She's a proud woman and now she's making up for her loss of face."

"She's a horrible bully," said Rose. "She bullies Aurora, and now you're letting her bully you. I bet she got you to give her a sovereign in compensation when she probably only had a sixpence in her purse. I'd stake a month of fish suppers that woman's a hundred times more dishonest than Effie."

"Rose, just at the moment I *need* her and Aurora. You can't deny it; the Infant Phenomenon is good for business."

"Maybe she is and maybe she isn't," said Rose darkly. "She's losing her confidence. You heard the crowd last night – more catcalls. Takings were down too. If the crowd get wind she's getting nervous, they'll start baiting her, and then she really will be in trouble."

Thomas nodded. He knew what Rose was saying was true. Aurora needed to change her act. Maybe he should have a word with Lizzie. He went to speak, but there were suddenly loud voices outside, exclamations of surprise and shock, and then the door burst open. Effie stumbled into the room followed by Grace Dorset and Freddie. Both were weeping. Grace's face was a pale blotch, and the shadows under her eyes were like bruises.

"Oh, Thomas," she cried. "It's Ned. He's dead. He's dead." She burst into noisy sobs, and Freddie set up such a wail that Rose scooped him into her arms.

"Dead?" said Thomas, putting an arm around Grace. "How? When?"

"I've just come from the morgue. I've seen him. Somebody cracked his skull open and threw my poor love in the river. I saw the wound on the back of his head with my own eyes. I kissed the butterfly birthmark on the nape of his neck."

Rose, who was still holding Freddie, flung her spare arm around Grace's heaving shoulders.

"My poor Ned has been lying all alone in the cold morgue for ten whole days," sobbed Grace. "If I hadn't found him he would have been given a pauper's funeral in an unmarked grave. I'd never have known what had happened to him."

"I'm so sorry, Gracie," said Thomas, taking the weeping woman into his arms. "Ten days is a long time to go without knowing where he was."

Rose had been thinking of the last time she saw Ned, in the Campion's gallery. She gasped.

"But I saw Ned ten days ago. It was the same day Aurora and Lizzie Gawkin turned up!"

"What time was this, Rose?" asked Grace.

"It was in the early evening. O'Leary and I were doing the *King John* scene."

"Then you must be mistaken," whispered Grace sorrowfully. "Ned was pulled out of the river around noon. Within hours of saying goodbye to me and Freddie, he was murdered."

The room was choked with a dense silence.

"Then we won't rest until we've found out

103

who was responsible and why," said Rose.

Thomas Campion nodded grimly in agreement.

13

"I did see him, I'm sure I did. Or else I'm going mad and should be put in an asylum," said Rose tearfully. "I didn't imagine it, honest. Ned was in the gallery. I know he was."

"Did you tell the rozzers?" asked Effie.

Rose nodded scornfully.

"Thomas and I went to see them yesterday, but I don't know why we bothered for all the notice they took. They've decided that Ned was so upset about not being able to get work that he flung himself into the river, hit his head and drowned." She added bitterly, "Case closed."

Rose viciously spun the pedal on the bicycle that Effie was holding.

"They were almost as bad as Lizzie Gawkin," she said angrily.

The news of Ned Dorset's death had upset everyone at Campion's. He'd been a great favourite among the ballet girls, and all the acts who'd known him were devastated. Apart from Lizzie Gawkin. She had complained loudly that all the weeping and wailing was giving her a headache. When Rose heard this, she shouted at the astonished Lizzie, telling her that she was a vulture and that Ned had been part of the Campion's family, which was more than Lizzie would ever be.

Lizzie had shrugged and given a vile little laugh. "Who wants to be part of this 'family'?" she cried. "I'm not going to weep for Ned Dorset; I never even met the man. I have no interest in him. He's nothing to me." She'd stood up and beckoned to Aurora. "Come, my treasure, we're going to the Four Cripples. My nerves are shredded."

As Lizzie pushed Aurora towards the door, Rose saw the tears in the girl's eyes as she mouthed, "I'm so sorry."

* ✻ *

Rose turned the pedal again on the bicycle. If she could find a way to work it into an act it would be a real novelty. Maybe it would attract a crowd. So far her sheep idea had failed to come to anything; she'd stood on London Bridge for two whole days and had been unable to persuade a single farmer to lend her his sheep.

"What was Ned doing when you saw him?" asked Effie, flicking a speck off the bike frame, which she had painted bright green with yellow daisies. It looked like the most cheerful thing in the whole of London.

Rose told her about Ned miming holding a baby and pointing at her. "I'm sure he was trying to tell me something."

"Maybe you saw Ned's ghost?" said Effie. "Maybe the ghost couldn't rest until he had told you something very important."

Rose was about to laugh when she stopped. She'd never been one for believing in ghosts, but now Effie had mentioned it she wondered if it could be true. It made her all the more certain that Ned had been murdered, and his ghost had returned to tell her something important. "Let's think about what we know so far." She ticked the information off on her fingers. "Grace told us that Ned left that morning saying he was coming to see Thomas, and that then he might have to go north. She also told us that he'd been north before on some kind of mysterious family mission. And that morning Ned got a letter from America, the second one he'd had."

"What happened to the letter?"

"Grace said he took it with him, and the police found something sodden and unreadable in his pocket when they pulled him out of the river."

"So he can't have been killed for the letter then," said Effie. "The murderer would've taken it, else."

Rose nodded and blinked back angry tears. Who could have wanted to kill Ned Dorset?

Sighing, she tightened another nut on the bicycle and turned to Effie. "Do you want to give it a turn around the yard?" she asked.

Effie shook her head shyly. "I don't know how," she said.

"It's easy," said Rose, and she hoiked up her skirts and started pedalling round the yard like a mad thing. She came to a sudden stop next to Effie. "Here, jump on the crossbar!"

With peals of laughter, Effie managed to clamber on and they wobbled off, shrieking and giggling.

Rose saw Aurora watching them wistfully. "Fancy a go?" she asked, trying and failing to make a dignified stop.

Aurora blushed pink with pleasure. "I'd love—"

But Lizzie suddenly appeared at her arm and pulled her away. "Come, my treasure," she said loudly. "I don't want you mixing with nasty common girls."

Rose snorted with laughter and yelled loudly, "Right, Effie! Let's see just how fast us nasty common girls can go."

Effie giggled, and then yelled, "Watch out!"

The butcher's boy had wandered into the yard and was so mesmerised by the sight of Rose's knickerbockers that he stood frozen to the spot. There was a loud crash, and Rose, Effie and the butcher's boy collapsed in a heap on the ground with the bicycle on top of them.

"Is anyone hurt?" asked Rose cheerfully.

"No," chorused Effie and the butcher's boy.

"You're as mad as a hatter, Rose Campion," said the butcher's boy. But there was more than a touch of admiration in his voice.

They were all still laughing when Grace appeared at the stage door. Everyone scrambled to their feet at the sight of her wan face.

"Sorry, Grace," said Rose, feeling they were

being insensitive. "We were making far too much noise."

Grace shook her head. "The world doesn't stop because my Ned is dead. I like to hear your laughter. Are you and Lottie still planning to take Freddie to see the mudlarks later?"

Grace and Freddie had been staying at Campion's for a few days now, and Lottie and the other ballet girls had made a pet of him. Rose had once walked into the dressing room to find them teaching him the cancan.

"Of course, Grace," said Rose. Grace smiled and went back inside.

"Poor Grace," said Effie. "She doesn't deserve this. My mum always said Grace, Ned and Freddie were the nicest people in the street. She thought Ned Dorset was a real gent."

Rose looked up from where she'd been tinkering with the bike, surprised. "I didn't know you knew Grace? And I didn't think you had any family."

Effie flushed. "I don't," she said hesitantly. "She died. I don't like to talk about it."

"I'm sorry. Must have been very recent," said Rose softly.

Effie looked away. Rose sensed something

evasive in her manner. But Campion's was full of people with secrets, people who wanted to reinvent themselves, or who had run away, or who didn't even know their own history. Like her. Rose knew it was best not to ask too many questions, and wait for people to reveal themselves if and when they chose to do so.

"Sorry, Effie," she said good-naturedly. "I didn't mean to pry. I'd better get back to work."

Effie watched as Rose wheeled the bicycle towards the stage door and into the theatre for safe keeping. She felt so guilty for saying her mum was dead when she wasn't. But she couldn't tell about her mum being in Holloway. She couldn't bear the thought of being turned away from Campion's.

A terrible thought occurred to her. What if by telling a lie about her mum, she was making something terrible come true? Maybe her mum *would* die suddenly. A tear spilled from her eye.

"I'm sorry, Mum. Forgive me. I didn't mean it. Please, please don't die," she whispered.

14

Lizzie Gawkin made her way through the swirling fog, stepping as delicately as she could to avoid the piles of dung being collected by armies of children swarming across the cobbles. They were going to dry the dung and take it to the tanning factories in Bermondsey.

Lizzie was wrapped up in a cloak, with a hat decorated with a tiny stuffed bird perched on her head. But she had the look less of a woman trying to defend herself from the icy wind and the smuts from the factory chimneys, and more like one eager to avoid recognition. Every now and again she stopped and looked furtively behind her to check she wasn't being followed, but it was hard to tell in a street so clotted with fog that people suddenly appeared and disappeared like apparitions.

She kept to the very edge of the street, hard up against the tipsy houses, moving stealthily like a scuttling rat. Occasionally a gap in the fog would open up and Lizzie's jowly features would be revealed in a sudden beam of thin sunlight. Once she narrowly avoided having the contents of a chamber pot land on her head from a window above.

Crossing London Bridge, she scurried on westwards where the narrow streets grew broader and the houses grander. She stopped in a square in Soho and consulted a piece of paper that she took from her pocket. Number twenty-four was over in one corner, a tall, narrow building whose upper floors lurched towards its neighbours as if seeking help to remain upright.

Lizzie had been excited when she had received the curt reply, acknowledging the letter she had sent on her arrival in Southwark. She had been impatient at the silence that then followed, and she had wondered if the bait hadn't been taken. Yesterday another letter had come, this time asking her to come to the offices of Snetherbridge and Skimpole in Soho Square.

The address had disappointed her. She'd expected the lawyers for Lord Henry Easingford to have offices in a more salubrious part of London. She glanced around nervously once more. Maybe it was a trap? She looked from side to side but could see nobody and nothing suspicious. Some children ran squealing across the square chasing pigeons. A flower seller was flirting with an organ grinder. A man in a bowler hat was sitting on a bench in the square, reading a newspaper that obscured his face. She took a deep breath and walked up the steps of number twenty-four. A brass plaque on the wall reassured her she was in the right place. She pulled the bell, and the damp swollen door was eventually pulled open by a pimply youth who was stooped like a sapling buffeted by the wind.

"Good day," said Lizzie grandly. "I am Mrs Gawkin, here to see Mr Snetherbridge."

"This way, madam. Mr Snetherbridge is expecting you." The youth closed the door and as he did so the bowler-hatted man put down his newspaper and walked slowly towards number twenty-four. At the railings he went down the steps and into the basement, whistling

"Pop Goes the Weasel" as he went.

Lizzie followed the stooped young man down a dark hall. The pimples on the back of his neck were raw and angry. He showed her into a small room dominated by a large desk. Behind this sat a large man with lustrous dark hair and whiskers who was wearing a funereal suit, rather the worse for snuff stains. His bright-yellow necktie made him look as if a dead canary had taken up residence around his neck.

The man rose to his feet and nodded to the boy, who retreated from the room. Walking around the side of the desk, he briefly extended his snuff-stained hand to Lizzie and snatched it away again quickly as if he feared contagion. He then ushered her towards an upright wooden chair on the other side of the desk. The chair's hardness was barely alleviated by a worn, dusky-pink velvet cushion.

"Do sit down, Mrs Gawkin," he said in silky tones. "Let's get straight down to business, shall we?"

Lizzie felt aggrieved. At the very least, she had expected to be relieved of her cloak and bonnet. She had even hoped to meet Lord Henry Easingford himself, who would quickly appreciate the quality and significance of her information. But she suspected that his lordship was nowhere near Soho Square, and that Mr Snetherbridge was not one of his lordship's regular lawyers, who no doubt resided in fragrant airy offices decked with Chinese silk wallpaper in St James's. Mr Snetherbridge, she surmised, was someone who was employed to deal with his lordship's less salubrious business. Well, she would surprise his lordship yet, and make him take her seriously. She gave the lawyer her sickliest smile.

"Of course, Mr Snetherbridge. I am here to help the Easingford family in any way I can."

Mr Snetherbridge looked pointedly at his pocket watch. "I have another meeting shortly, Mrs Gawkin, so I'm afraid I must hurry things along. In your letter, you said you believe there is another with a claim to the estate of Lord Easingford, and that you have some proof that this person is alive. I would like to make clear that my client, Lord Henry, is sure you are mistaken."

Lizzie gave a simpering cough. "What an honour it must be for his lordship – an appointment to the Privy Council by our dear

116

Queen! And what a shame if there were to be any nasty rumours flying about…"

The lawyer's face hardened. "And what rumours would those be, Mrs Gawkin?"

Lizzie narrowed her eyes. "That there was a child. Born to his brother's wife, Lily Easingford, six months after the death of Lord Frederick. A son. Heir to the Easingford title and estate, and to his mother's fortune. A child that makes Lord Henry a usurper both of the title and of Lily Easingford's wealth."

"But the child didn't live, Mrs Gawkin, as everybody knows. Edward Frederick Dorset Easingford was stillborn and has been buried in the Easingford churchyard with his mother for the last thirty-two years."

Lizzie smiled sweetly. "Now, Mr Snetherbridge, you and I both know that isn't true."

Mr Snetherbridge rose. "What utter nonsense, Mrs Gawkin. Thank you for your time but I don't think we have anything else to discuss."

Lizzie leaned forward and hissed across the desk. "Don't be so hasty, Mr Snetherbridge. What if the child didn't die? What if the coffin maker and his wife took Edward away for safekeeping? And if they took with them a silver cup bearing the Easingford crest and a blue ribbon that had been placed in the coffin with that child. What if Edward grew up and then had a child of his own? Like the father, any such child would have a legal claim against Lord Henry's estate." Lizzie sat back, her hand pressed dramatically to her heart. "Oh, Mr Snetherbridge! Just think of the scandal! The Easingford family name would be blackened forever if it ever came out that he had robbed his brother's descendants of their true inheritance."

Mr Snetherbridge had resumed his seat but he looked unruffled. "This is a fine story, Mrs Gawkin, and you tell it well. But without proof, that's all it is. A likely story."

Lizzie reached into her bag and pulled out a blue ribbon. "But, Mr Snetherbridge, isn't that why I'm here?"

The lawyer leaned forward to look at the ribbon, not quite so unruffled this time. "Is there anything more?"

From the depths of her bag Lizzie pulled a piece of paper. On it was a drawing of a silver cup engraved with the Easingford crest.

Mr Snetherbridge reached for the drawing but

Lizzie kept it safely out of his way. "And you have the cup?" he asked.

Lizzie smiled slyly as she put the ribbon and paper back into her bag. "Not on me, of course. I'm not stupid. It's somewhere safe and the written account of its provenance is kept with it." Lizzie touched her nose knowingly. "My insurance, just in case things get nasty."

Mr Snetherbridge rose to his feet for a second time.

"Mrs Gawkin, I must talk to my client. It might be that we could see our way to making you some kind of payment for the return of the cup and ribbon, not of course because we believe that your story is anything other than balderdash, but because – if they prove to be genuine – they are part of my client's family heritage, a heritage that he values. The story is, of course, a fabrication. Edward Easingford was stillborn. He cannot have had a child of his own. That is the end of the matter."

Mrs Gawkin's eyes glittered. "If you say so, Mr Snetherbridge. But I know what I know. Edward lived and is in fact only recently deceased; his child is alive and well, and ready to make public a claim to be recognised as the direct descendant of the rightful Lord Easingford." She paused. "And with Lord Easingford about to be made a member of the Privy Council..." She coughed delicately. "How unfortunate would it be if anything came to light to scupper that appointment?"

Mrs Gawkin stood and faced the lawyer.

"But have it your own way, Mr Snetherbridge. I have been patient for a while now, and I can be patient a while longer."

Mr Snetherbridge rang a small brass bell on his desk and the pimply youth reappeared to usher Lizzie out. At the door, she turned and gave a fox-like grin. "Good day, Mr Snetherbridge. I shall wait to hear from you."

As soon as he heard the front door slam shut behind her, Lord Henry Easingford – forbidding as an eagle and greying around the temples – stepped out from behind a curtained recess in his lawyer's office.

"Damn that woman!" he spat. "When she sent that blasted letter, I thought it was just a shot in the dark. How the devil did she get hold of that ribbon and cup? We must find them. And then we shall have to deal with her. But at the moment she's more useful alive than dead. We need to keep watching her, see if there is anyone else involved. She might be part of a conspiracy. Check out her story. If my nephew did survive, we need to find him. If he's recently dead, as Gawkin suggests, we need to find his brat. There may be a wife too, who will need to be dealt with. Get Josiah Pinch to report back on where Lizzie Gawkin goes and who she talks to."

Lord Easingford began to pace the room. "If my nephew did survive, why did he not come forward years ago?"

"I don't know, m'lud. Maybe because Edward didn't live and this is just the fantasy of a common blackmailer. We will only know for sure if the objects she claims to have prove to be genuine. Your son, Edgar, is the estate and title's only heir as far as the law is concerned."

"Ha!" Lord Henry gave a mirthless laugh. "And what news, Snetherbridge, of the ungrateful young pup?"

"My informants tell me that he remains in America, m'lud. Still an actor, m'lud." Mr Snetherbridge said the word "actor" as if he held it in a pair of tweezers. "About to play Hamlet in Chicago, so I hear."

His lordship looked unimpressed.

"Play-acting! And for twelve years now. He has too much of Sarah in him. She always was the spirited one of the two sisters; my poor brother chose better when he married Lily." Lord Henry stopped pacing and turned to his lawyer, who flinched at the dark look on his face. "I will settle this business, and then we will reel young Edgar in. He must face up to his responsibilities as my son and heir. Everything I have done, I have done for him, and it is time he became the true custodian of Easingford."

Mr Snetherbridge watched as Lord Henry resumed his pacing. It was as though his lordship had forgotten he was in the room and was talking to himself.

"The vixen knows something, but does she know everything? The coffin maker and his wife disappeared the day Lily and her dratted babe were buried. I thought they were just fleeing the influenza. If I'd thought there was anything more significant to their disappearance, I'd have hounded them down long ago." He shook his head. "No. The child was as lifeless as his mother. I made quite sure of that."

Mr Snetherbridge blinked at what he was hearing but Lord Henry seemed oblivious to his own confession. The lawyer cleared his throat. "Of course, there is a way to check if there is any truth at all in the story."

"What do you mean?"

There was a pause. "Well, we could dig up the coffin."

Lord Henry stared. "But on what grounds would a judge grant us an exhumation order? Besides, it would cause more unwelcome gossip."

Mr Snetherbridge blinked very fast. "I was thinking of something a little more discreet, m'lud. Maybe something not altogether legal. A private uncoffining, as it were. I could provide the means and it might set your mind at rest."

His lordship stared at the other man thoughtfully as he threw a glossy black astrakhan coat around his shoulders. "That might be a very good suggestion," he said. "Summon Josiah Pinch. Tell him to watch Lizzie Gawkin like a hawk, see if he can trace the coffin maker and his wife, and keep his ear to the ground for any rumours about the existence of my nephew. Oh, and, Snetherbridge, pay him well. I don't want him turning blackmailer. He's a nasty piece of work."

The lawyer watched his lordship leave the room, before ringing the bell. *You're a pretty nasty piece of work yourself, Lord Henry*, he thought. *But you pay well.*

There was a knock on the door and the boy appeared. "Fetch Josiah Pinch," the lawyer barked.

15

Effie slipped through the labyrinth of narrow streets as if she had known them all her life. She was on her way back to Campion's after fetching some more bolts and screws for Thomas. The two of them were working together to mend the long disused tunnel above the stage where metal balls could be run from one end to the other to create the sound of thunder. Thomas thought a thunder-run would bring in more customers, and Campion's certainly needed them.

"If we get it working," Thomas said, "we can have O'Leary going mad on the blasted heath in *King Lear*. Or if the gin has addled his brain too much, maybe I'll play the role myself."

Effie frowned. She didn't know who on earth

King Lear was and she didn't like the sound of a blasted heath.

"Rosie said you used to be an actor?" she asked, finding it hard to imagine the sensible Thomas swaggering about on stage. She still found all the performers at Campion's romantic and exotic figures. Thomas, who always had a twinkle in his eye, didn't fit that picture at all.

"I was, a long time ago. And a playwright too. That's how I made the money to buy Campion's. Writing melodramas. If we get the thunder-run working, Effie, I'll write us a new play featuring lots of thunder and lightning." He grinned wickedly. "Or perhaps we could put on a scene from *Macbeth* with Lizzie Gawkin playing one of the three witches."

Effie's eyes grew round. "What's *Macbeth*?" she asked.

"It's a play by Shakespeare," said Thomas, "about a man who so wants to be king that he will go to any lengths to get the crown and keep it, even if it destroys him."

"Rose is always going on 'bout Shakespeare," said Effie. "She said she'd teach me to read but I don't see the point. Reading's not for the likes of me." She added proudly: "But I did let Rose teach me how to ride the bicycle, and she said I was a natural."

"Would you like to try performing, Effie?" asked Thomas. "Maybe you could get Rosie to help you work up an act?"

Effie blushed. "I'm too shy. I like doing things with me hands."

"You've got nifty little fingers, all right," said Thomas cheerfully. "If the theatre doesn't work out, you could always consider prigging." He looked up from the nail he was hammering and saw her expression, her eyes dark in a chalky face. "I'm sorry, Effie. I wasn't thinking."

"S'all right," mumbled Effie. "Lizzie Gawkin thinks the same."

"No one cares what Lizzie Gawkin thinks," said Thomas firmly. "Just you remember that."

Now Effie was working her way through the streets, eager to finish the thunder-run. The frozen fog had cleared and there was a touch of warmth in the pale sun.

"Home," she said out loud, and there was such a skip in her step that the hawkers and errand boys smiled at her as she passed, and children ran after her trying to sell her a penny sparkler or a ribbon. But as she got nearer the river, the fog descended again and coated everything in its eerie yellow glow.

Effie slipped down an alley and had almost reached the end when a figure wearing a bowler loomed out of the murk and seized her by the wrist.

"Hello, sweetheart," said the man, his face so close she could smell fetid breath and feel the tickle of his slug-like waxed moustache on her cheek.

"Josiah!" squeaked Effie in fear.

"Long time, no see," said Josiah, raising his hat mockingly. "Tell me that you've missed me, Effie." She tried to wriggle out of his grip but he held her tight in his grasp. "I hear you're living at Campion's."

"Who told yer? How'd you find me?" demanded Effie.

"Oh, I have eyes and ears everywhere. Don't think that you can ever escape me."

"Leave me alone!" shouted Effie.

"I will, Effie, I will. I've no real interest in you, you're just a sprat. But a sprat can be used to catch a mackerel. I need you to do a little job for me."

Effie's eyes blazed. "I ain't doing nowt for you!"

Josiah tightened his grip on her wrist and Effie winced at the pain.

"You will, my girl," he drawled. "Because if you don't, it will be the worse for you and that mother of yours. What if new information was discovered about her crimes? That she wasn't just a poor woman taking her chance when temptation came her way but that she was a hardened criminal instead? Do you think the judge would show her such leniency then?" He laughed darkly and mimicked drawing a knife across his throat.

"You wouldn't dare!"

"Oh, Effie! Effie! You know me better than that. Of course I would."

"What do you want me to do?" whispered Effie.

"It's very simple, sweetheart. I need you to be my eyes and ears. Lizzie Gawkin – I want you to listen out for anything she says, any gossip about her, anyone who comes to visit."

Effie felt relief. She feared that Josiah would want her to spy on Thomas. She had wondered whether Thomas might be in debt to the same person who had owned the Shoreditch tenement where she and her mother had lived.

"Nobody likes her. She don't have any visitors," said Effie, hoping it would be enough.

"But people come and go. I've been watching."

"Course they do, it's a music hall, ain't it."

"Less of your lip, sweetheart," said Josiah. "What about that pale woman I've seen? With the kid. Little boy? I've seen him through the fence playing in the yard. She's always dressed in black."

"Grace? She's got nothing to do with Lizzie Gawkin," said Effie. "Thomas Campion has taken her in because her husband was murdered."

Josiah smirked. "How very careless of him."

"I hate you!" cried Effie, trying to pull away from him. "Everyone says Ned Dorset was a good man, and he was murdered and flung in the Thames. You're a pig for laughing."

Josiah cocked his head at her words and frowned. What was it old Snetherbridge had said? Keep an ear out for anyone called Edward Frederick Dorset Easingford, or anything like it.

"Dorset, you say? Ned Dorset?" He

130

applied more pressure to Effie's wrist so that the skin burned and the pain was unbearable. Effie nodded, desperate to get away. "And what's the kid called?"

"Freddie."

Josiah gave a quick little smile. Ned Dorset must be the fellow Mr Snetherbridge and his lordship had been so keen to track down. So this Edward, or Ned, as he was calling himself, was dead. But there was a son, Freddie!

"Listen, Effie," said Josiah. "You're going to do a job for me. I want you to find some things that Lizzie Gawkin has got and that I want."

"What?" asked Effie listlessly.

"A silver cup and a blue ribbon."

"I can't," said Effie. "She and Aurora have their own dressing room. There's no reason for me to go in there."

"Then make one up," said Josiah. "And when you have, find the cup and the ribbon and bring them to me."

Effie's eyes widened with horror. "You want me to steal them?"

Josiah smiled nastily. "Once a thief, always a thief, eh?"

"And if I do, you'll leave me be?"

"Of course, sweetheart." He paused. "But if you don't, it will be bad news for your mother. She'll grow old in the clink. If she's lucky…"

Josiah Pinch watched Effie slip away, her head low and her shoulders hunched. He smiled. She had no idea how much she had helped him already.

16

Aurora heaved Lizzie into the bed and waited patiently to make quite sure that she had sunk into a deep sleep. For the last few days Lizzie had been in an unexpectedly good mood, walking around with a little smirk on her face as if she knew something. It made Aurora nervous. Twice she had heard Lizzie asking O'Leary if a letter had come for her. Every afternoon she took Aurora with her to the Four Cripples, where she worked her way through a jug of gin in record time.

"My ship's about to come in," she crowed as she jabbed Aurora in the chest with a pudgy finger. She took another swig of gin. "Lizzie Gawkin knows how to play the long game. More than twelve years I've waited for this. Twelve years of slumming it in the halls. But it won't be much longer and then I'll get all I deserve." She signalled to Aurora to pour more gin, but the jug was empty. Aurora braced herself to be pinched and sworn at, but instead Lizzie tried to stand up. For a moment she swayed like a tree in a high wind and then she fell to the floor, dead drunk.

It was a struggle to pick her up and lug her to the lodging house but Aurora managed in the end. She wanted Lizzie away from Campion's. This was her chance to get a good look in the trunk, see if she could find any clues to her history in that little box Lizzie guarded so closely.

With any luck the woman would sleep right through tonight's performances and she wouldn't have to face her constant criticism when she came off stage, or the pinching and poking that went with it. Lizzie's drinking was getting worse, and it was making her ever more unpleasant. Aurora knew that Rose had noticed her bruised arms but she'd kept her mouth shut. Any interference was sure to make Lizzie worse, not better.

Lizzie had been talking about moving to a

music hall in Blackfriars, which had a terrible reputation. Aurora knew she'd be eaten alive by a Blackfriars audience. At least at Campion's, Thomas ran a tight ship. But she knew her old act was no longer drawing in the crowds. She wouldn't be surprised if he didn't renew her contract at the end of the week.

Aurora waited by Lizzie's bed, itching to get to Campion's. She wanted to make quite sure that there was no chance Lizzie would awaken. She looked down at the comatose woman and felt nothing but repulsion. Aurora had never had a family but she had seen from the way people treated each other at Campion's what family meant, and the way Lizzie treated her didn't feel anything like that. Well, she was going to find out once and for all if Lizzie was her aunt or not, and if she wasn't, she was going to throw herself on Thomas Campion's mercy. He was always kind to her.

When she was quite certain that Lizzie was dead to the world she snaffled the keys from her pocket and made her way to the music hall. She didn't have long before she was due on stage for her first slot of the evening.

Campion's was unusually busy today. Some

workmen had been in to help the stagehands mend the trap beneath the stage. As Aurora slipped in by the stage door, a number of delivery boys were entering or leaving, entirely unnoticed by the dozing O'Leary.

Aurora headed straight to the dressing room. She took a last peep into the corridor before she shut the door. She saw Effie's retreating back, and guessed she'd been dropping off some costumes in the ballet girls' room next door. All clear.

After a quick change into her costume, Aurora got out the keys and glanced anxiously towards the door again, as if expecting Lizzie to come charging in any second.

"Don't be such a ninny, Aurora," she said to herself. Lizzie was certain to be snoring in the lodging house for a good few hours yet. Quickly she opened the trunk and peered inside. She took out the small lacquered box, unlocked it and took out a small silver cup and ribbon. She examined the cup and saw the pretty butterfly crest and words in Latin that she didn't understand. She looked closer at the crest and saw the name Easingford underneath. For a moment she allowed her mind to drift. Maybe she had something to do with the Easingford family. Maybe she was a long-lost baby, snatched from the bosom of her loving family by Lizzie Gawkin. She sighed. If only.

Setting the cup aside, Aurora pulled out some papers in the box. She riffled through them and quickly realised with disgust that Lizzie Gawkin was a blackmailer. She appeared to have been blackmailing somebody at almost every hall they had passed through. Aurora began to hope more than ever she'd find proof that Lizzie Gawkin was not her aunt. She couldn't bear to be related to such a despicable person.

She saw a sheet of headed notepaper and pulled it out. There was another crest at the top, a different one this time, with flowery letters entwined together. Underneath were the words *Ivanhoe House Asylum, Balham*. She was about to read on when she heard an all too familiar screech coming down the corridor.

"Aurora! Oh, where is the little brat!"

The girl's heart skipped a beat. She couldn't be discovered going through the trunk! She just hoped that Lizzie hadn't realised her keys were missing.

"Aurora! Aurora!" Lizzie's voice, which

carried like broken bagpipes, was coming nearer. Aurora locked the lacquered box, stuffed it back in the trunk and slammed the lid shut. She fumbled with the keys and they fell on the floor. She snatched them up and stuffed them in the pocket of her costume.

"Aurora!"

She had to stop Lizzie coming into the room, in case seeing the trunk made her reach for her keys and realise they were missing. She opened the door and ran into the corridor. Lizzie was weaving her way along, obviously still very much the worse for wear. She wasn't wearing her bonnet and gloves, and her hair was falling out of its bun.

"I'm here! I'm just coming, Auntie," said Aurora, taking Lizzie's arm and trying to steer her back towards the stage door. Lizzie frowned. Even in her sozzled state she recognised that Aurora calling her Auntie was unusual.

"What have you been doing?" she demanded suspiciously.

"Just getting myself ready to go on stage," replied Aurora, her eyes as wide as a newborn lamb. "Come on, let's get you settled where you can watch or I'll miss my cue."

She eased Lizzie into a chair at the side of the stage. Aurora knew she had plenty of time. Molly was just finishing her act, and then there would be a Dutch-doll dance sequence before she was due on. Aurora listened to the crowd. They were unusually raucous for so early in the day, and were being whipped into a frenzy of excitement by Molly's swirling skirts and a glimpse of knickerbockers and ankle. But Aurora had other things to worry about. If she could just get Lizzie to stay in the chair perhaps she would doze off again, and she would be able to race back to the dressing room, lock the trunk and put the keys back in Lizzie's pocket before she woke up again.

Lizzie's eyes rolled. She slumped back and gave a snore so loud that even Molly, who had come to a rest, heard it above the crowd. She looked their way and gave Aurora a wink. Aurora bit her lip. She needed to return to the dressing room and lock the trunk. Lizzie gave another stuttering snore and jerked awake. She looked around dazed. Then she patted her pocket. "My keys! Where are my keys?"

Aurora made a split-second decision. She reached into her pocket deftly and bent down as if looking under the chair.

"Here they are," she said brightly. "They must have dropped under your chair." Lizzie grabbed them and pushed them down deep in her pocket just as Molly brushed by, shaking her head and muttering grimly, "'Orrible crowd, but at least they let me live. Just. You'll need your wits out there tonight, love."

The chorus ran on from the other side of the stage, all dressed as Dutch dolls, and started twirling wildly so that their skirts and blonde plaits went flying. The crowd seemed to like this display and settled again.

Lizzie had gone back to sleep and didn't stir. Aurora wondered whether she had time to filch the keys again, lock the trunk and stuff them back in Lizzie's pocket without her realising. It was risky. Aurora hesitated, and the chance was lost as Rose appeared to watch the dancers from the side of the stage. Rose was sure to notice her taking the keys off Lizzie. She'd just have to hope that in her inebriated state Lizzie wouldn't realise that the trunk was unlocked. Or that she'd assume she left it that way herself. The doll dance was coming to an end. Aurora readied herself to step into the heat and glare of the lights and face the audience beyond.

* ✱ *

Effie slipped past the half-open door of the ballet dancers' dressing room and heard the laughter from inside. Not all the girls were in the Dutch-doll routine. One of the girls, Tess, was being teased about a stage-door admirer who sent her flowers every day.

"Lor, Tess," said Lottie. "Tell him to stop sending lilies. It's like a ruddy funeral parlour in 'ere. Stick that lot on that table; I can't move for flowers over 'ere."

Effie paused, and almost turned back again as she had already done three times this afternoon. Twice she'd lost her nerve halfway down the corridor, and once she had got as far as the door of Lizzie Gawkin's dressing room before realising that someone was in there. Each failure had felt strangely like a relief.

But it was now or never. Lizzie was slumped drunkenly asleep in her chair at the side of the stage, and even if she did wake she'd stay to watch Aurora, who was about to go on stage. Effie had one of Aurora's shawls over her arm, just back from the laundry. If anyone found her in the dressing room she could say she'd been delivering it, even though Aurora usually picked up her own laundry parcel from the stage door.

She didn't want to steal anything but doing nothing was not an option. She knew that Josiah's threats were never idle. A quick glance behind her, and then she pushed the door of the dressing room and stepped inside.

The trunk was in the middle of the room. Effie tried the lid and to her surprise it opened. She rummaged about, but there was no sign of a silver cup or ribbon, just a small lacquered box. Trembling, she tried the lid. It was locked. Maybe this was what Josiah wanted? Maybe the cup and ribbon were inside and that's why it was locked. It was better than nothing.

She crept to the door, the box concealed under the shawl, and walked down the corridor. She slipped into the props room and buried the lacquered box inside a trunk full of *Aladdin* panto stuff. Nobody would find it there and she could come back and get it later. She crammed the shawl on top too.

Effie joined Rose at the side of the stage to watch Aurora, holding her hands tightly together to stop them from trembling. As soon as she had left the box in the props room, she'd regretted taking it. She should just have made something up to tell Josiah and hoped he didn't carry out his threats. Maybe there was still time to retrieve the box and return it to the trunk?

She went to leave, but Rose slipped her arm through hers. Now she felt even worse. Rose and Thomas had welcomed her into the Campion's family and she was betraying them by stealing. She dropped her arm from Rose's. She would retrieve the box and put it back and nobody would ever know. Maybe she could tell Thomas about Josiah. She felt certain he would know what to do. No, she couldn't, because she'd have to admit she had been a thief. She turned to leave but Rose, who was watching the stage intently, put a restraining hand on her wrist.

"Aurora's in trouble out there," she said. "We need to get her off."

Effie realised she had been so lost in her own thoughts that she hadn't appreciated what a rough time Aurora was having. She was doing one of her most simpering turns and the crowd had no patience with it. Aurora kept faltering, the musicians kept looking for the signal to stop, but the girl would plough on regardless. The crowd were really shouting at her now, booing and braying.

Rose gestured wildly at Aurora to leave the stage, but she stayed, mesmerised, like a deer caught looking down the barrel of a poacher's gun. Aurora had stopped singing but she didn't move. She just stood in the glare, seemingly paralysed by fear. One of the stagehands took a step on to the stage to try and grab Aurora, but was greeted by a barrage of missiles. He retreated, knowing that if the crowd were roused further, there'd be a riot. The situation was already out of control.

"Where's Thomas?" he asked.

"Out." Rose shook her head helplessly. They needed him. Thomas could quell an audience merely by stepping on stage. The roar was getting louder. The ballet girls came tearing down the corridor.

"Oh, lor," said Lottie. "They're goin' to run riot. It 'appened at the Ledbury last year. Not a stick of furniture or a window that weren't broken. They 'ad to close for a month."

Even Lizzie had woken up and was looking around dazed as if she had no idea where she was.

More things were being thrown at the stage. Something hit Aurora on the side of the cheek and she swayed slightly, but still she stood there. The noise was getting louder. A chair was thrown, and then a glass.

"We've got to do something," said Rose desperately, "or they're going to break the whole place up. We need to give them something they've never seen before."

She suddenly turned to Effie. "Quick! Get the bicycle!"

Effie rushed off and was back in a twinkling with the brightly coloured bicycle covered with daisies. Rose hoiked up her skirts, jumped on and wobbled on to the stage. The musicians saw her coming and knew immediately what they should do. They broke very loudly into "Daisy Bell", a song that was still new enough to be fresh but which was also hugely popular. "Daisy, Daisy, give me your answer, do, I'm half crazy…"

It was an infectious song and one that the crowd all knew. Lottie and the others at the side of the stage belted out the chorus, "But you'll look sweet, upon the seat, of a bicycle built for two!" as Rose gathered speed and raced round the stage in circles. At one point she balanced on just one pedal with her other leg straight out behind her like a ballerina. It caught the crowd's attention and they roared their approval, all the bad temper quickly evaporating.

Aurora stood looking at her as if waking from a bad dream. Rose brought the bicycle to a rest by her side, patted the crossbar and whispered, "Jump on! Here's your chance to be a nasty common girl! In public!"

Aurora hesitated for a split second, then grinned gratefully, lifted her skirts and leapt on. The two of them raced wildly around the stage, singing with such gaiety and abandon – punctuated by the odd shriek as Rose took a corner too fast – that the audience was utterly captivated. The crowd were on their feet, delirious with delight and thrilled at the sheer daring of two girls together on one bicycle.

Rose made one last circle as the musicians played the final rousing chorus and everyone joined in. Aurora tossed her hat into the crowd and Rose blew everyone a kiss as they cycled off the stage. Effie and the others in the wings were all watching open-mouthed and exhilarated. Rose put the brakes on a little too hard and both girls fell in a heap on the floor. The others helped them up. The crowd were screaming for more.

"Yer better get out there and take a bow," said Lottie.

Rose grabbed Aurora's hand and pulled her back on stage, eyes sparkling. They curtseyed and their pleasure in their unexpected success made the audience warm to them even more. The audience stamped and called for an encore. Rose held up a hand, and they fell obediently silent.

"We will be performing the act again in the second show tonight if you would all like to return. If you show your ticket for this performance you will get tuppence off."

Aurora looked astonished at this news, while the crowd sighed their disappointment that the girls weren't going to do an encore.

Rose put a finger to her lips and silenced them. "Now the act you've all been waiting for, the one and only, the amazing, the beautiful – Dolores! Put your hands together for the queen of the slack wire who will astonish you with her skill and beauty."

The audience cheered and settled down to watch. They liked Dolores; she could be quite saucy. Rose pulled Aurora off the stage where everyone showered them with praise. The ballet girls rushed away to change. Lizzie was nowhere to be seen. Effie looked around. Maybe this was her chance to replace the box in the trunk.

Aurora caught Rose's hand. "Thank you, Rose," she said. "You saved me out there."

Rose grinned. "Well, I wasn't just going to stand by and watch you being savaged. I know how lonely it can feel out there on the stage when things go wrong."

Aurora's eyes were damp. "You didn't have to do it. You could have left me there." She gulped. "Especially after how stand-offish I've been."

"All forgotten," said Rose. "Let's make a fresh start." She put out her hand. "Rose Campion," she said with a little bob.

Aurora took Rose's hand and curtseyed. "Aurora Scarletti."

The girls laughed. "Do you really mean for us to do it again later?" Aurora asked.

"Why not?" said Rose. "They loved it. We could even work it up into a proper act, give it a bit more structure."

"Lizzie might have something to say about that," said Aurora doubtfully.

Rose shrugged. "She might. But if there's money in it, I doubt she'll complain. I'll talk to Thomas—" She broke off at a scream that came from the other end of the corridor.

"I've been robbed!" shrieked Lizzie. "I've been robbed!"

People came running, including Thomas, who had just returned. Hanging back at the edge of the crowd, Effie felt her cheeks burning. She was sure her guilt was written all over her face. She blinked back tears; her chance to replace the box was gone. There was no going back now. Maybe Josiah was right. Once a thief, always a thief.

17

Cold gripped the desolate moorland churchyard in its iron teeth, and a bitter wind whipped around the gravestones. The clang of spades against the frozen earth echoed across the moor. A fox cried out somewhere, a painful unworldly sound that made Mr Snetherbridge shudder. He wished he was snug in bed at home in his suburban villa in Chiswick, where his garden was his pride and joy, not out here in a moonlit graveyard with Lord Easingford, as jumpy as a colt, by his side. He looked around at the ancient mausoleum and the Easingford gravestones – vast ornamental marble slabs – that marked the Easingford domain. Even in death the family dominated, pushing all the other graves over to the far side of the churchyard.

Beneath the sacking used to hide the names on it, the headstone of the grave being exhumed was a far plainer affair; a simple stone marked the final resting place of Lily Easingford and her stillborn son, Edward. Mr Snetherbridge stamped his feet, wondering why the family seemed to have selected the most windswept area of the graveyard for their final resting places. Nothing would grow and bloom in this bleak spot. He wondered why they hadn't chosen the area by the church that was clearly the only sunny spot in the whole blasted place. Oriental lilies stood to attention by the wall, under which was a small grassy knoll carpeted with wild daffodils. He preferred their other name, the Lent lily.

Mr Snetherbridge looked at Lord Henry, who shivered and pulled his astrakhan coat more tightly around him. A glance at his pocket watch told him it was past two o'clock. The very dead of night. Although the moon was bright, the two men Mr Snetherbridge had brought from London were working by the flickering light of two candlelit lamps. The sweat gleamed on their brows as they dug down into the darkness to find the coffin. They would be warmer still when they had been paid generously to keep their mouths shut, blindfolded and driven the forty-odd miles to the railway station on the edge of the city and dispatched back to London. If they were foolish enough to blab about the strange job they had undertaken they would be unable to identify its location.

At least his lordship would soon know if Lizzie Gawkin's story had any foundation. One of the men gave a low shout and Mr Snetherbridge saw them start to clear the soil from the top of the coffin. Mr Snetherbridge looked anxiously around. But who would be out on the moor on a desolate night like tonight? Even the parson, who Lord Easingford referred to as "that dratted busybody" would be safely asleep in his warm bed in the village vicarage. Only the bats and the owls would be there to bear witness. The coffin seemed to be remarkably intact, perhaps preserved by something in this hardy soil, and the men were now digging around the sides so they could slip a rope over either end to lift it to the surface.

At that moment there came the distant sound of a horse's hooves. There was a moment of panic. Mr Snetherbridge snuffed out the lamps and signalled to the men to retire into the porch of the church and stay hidden in the shadows. The horse drew nearer, steam rising from its body so for a moment it looked like a spectre from a ghost story, not a real live animal. Mr Snetherbridge signalled to the men to return to the grave and lift the coffin.

"It's only Josiah," he said.

"What on earth is he doing here?" snapped his lordship.

"I gave him instructions to come if he had any urgent news. He would only have come all this way if he had good reason," said Mr Snetherbridge soothingly. Josiah was securing the horse. A few large flakes of snow were beginning to swirl around like ghostly moths.

Lord Henry and Mr Snetherbridge turned their attention back to the open grave. The men were beginning to drag the coffin upwards. The wood creaked; in places it was rotted through and you could glimpse its dark, secretive shadows. Josiah joined them just as the men began to lever the coffin lid away. He opened his mouth to speak but Lord Easingford held up a hand to silence him. He didn't want his business discussed in front of the gravediggers, and he wanted to see inside the coffin. There was a creak as the men pulled the coffin lid away entirely. Everyone stared down into it. The coffin was completely empty.

For several seconds there was a blank, shocked silence. His lordship sank to the ground on one knee.

"This cannot be," he muttered, more to himself than anyone else. Then he recovered from the shock of the absence of the bodies of both Lily and the baby. His face was thunderous.

"The mother cannot have lived. Rigor mortis had set in – I saw it with my own eyes. The child... Maybe the child did live... Maybe I didn't—" He broke off. "What does this mean?"

Mr Snetherbridge took a nervous step backwards. "I don't know, m'lud," he said, and wiped the sweat off his top lip.

His lordship was pacing restlessly up and down. He had buried the woman and her child thirty-two years ago. He had seen the coffin lid hammered in place. He had been rid of them, or so he thought, and now three decades on they were returning to haunt him.

He nodded curtly at the hired men to return the coffin to the grave and start to cover it over.

It was beginning to snow quite heavily. Good. If they finished the job and left quickly, all evidence that they had disturbed the grave or even been there would be covered over. The job was swiftly done, and the workmen were taken by Mr Snetherbridge to a waiting coach further down the road, where they were given brandy and sent on their way.

Mr Snetherbridge returned to the graveside. Lord Easingford was staring at the plot as it fast became covered by snow. He had a look of complete bewilderment on his face, as if he was still looking into the empty coffin. Josiah had followed them, whistling as usual under his breath. Mr Snetherbridge frowned, and the younger man realised what he was doing and stopped.

His lordship turned to Josiah. "What news do you have? Good, I hope. Better than the news the night has brought so far."

Josiah licked his lips nervously. "The babe did live."

His lordship gave a hollow, angry laugh. "I think we've worked that out for ourselves."

"I know nothing about the mother; I have no news of her fate," said Josiah calmly. "But I have good news about her son. He is dead. Recently deceased, as Lizzie Gawkin suggested. Pulled from the river just a couple of weeks ago."

His lordship studied him sharply. "You are quite, quite certain of your information? That it was my nephew?"

Josiah nodded. "I have it from a most reliable source. Someone close to Lizzie Gawkin, but definitely not in her pay. He was an actor and music-hall performer, the usual kind of lowlife."

"How can you be sure it's him?"

"It fits: from everything Snetherbridge told me and that Lizzie Gawkin told you. But there's more. There's the name he was using." Josiah couldn't resist giving a dramatic little pause. "Ned Dorset."

His lordship's eyes widened and he nodded. "Promising. Very promising. I care nothing for the mother, Lily, although her absence from the coffin is puzzling. It was the existence of the son I feared. But you are confirming what Lizzie Gawkin said, that he is dead…"

"There's more, sir," said Josiah. "Lizzie Gawkin said that Edward had a child and she's right. Ned Dorset, as he was calling himself, was married and had a son of his own."

"And is that child alive or dead?"

"Very much alive and currently residing with his mother, the widow Grace, at Campion's Palace of Varieties and Wonders. Until recently, the family were living in Shoreditch on the other side of the street from the tenements that you own, m'lud."

"And what is the son called?" enquired Mr Snetherbridge.

"Freddie. Short for Frederick Dorset," said Josiah with a flourish.

"Does the wife know her deceased husband's history?" asked his lordship sharply.

"I can't say," said Josiah. "I am still gathering information. I have someone who I have every confidence will provide me with the silver cup, the ribbon and perhaps more. Maybe even some documents."

"Good work, Josiah," said Mr Snetherbridge. He turned to his lordship. "What is to be done with this Grace and Freddie Dorset?"

"Deal with them as you did my wife, Sarah. It will eliminate the immediate threat that Grace Dorset might start blabbing, and we can make a longer-term plan when we have discovered how much of her husband's history she knows.

Tell me when it is done. Oh, and one more thing: when you have the child, I want you to tell me if he has any kind of birthmark. That may be all the conclusive proof we need."

"What kind of mark, m'lud?"

"A butterfly. The emblem of the Easingford family. Generations of Easingford children have borne one. Almost always situated on the nape of the neck, but not always in that location. I have one; my son has it too. My brother bore one, and so did his son, Edward, so if this Freddie Dorset is a true Easingford it's likely he bears one as well. Now, we must leave while the snow will still cover our tracks."

They disappeared into the night while the snow continued to fall, covering the graveyard and all that had taken place in it in a thick, white shroud.

18

It was raining in the quiet London churchyard where Ned Dorset was being buried. Rose stood at the open graveside as the coffin was lowered, holding tightly to Freddie's small hand. His sobbing mother held his other hand, supported by Thomas.

Apart from Lizzie Gawkin, who had taken to her bed since the robbery, the whole of Campion's had turned out for the service and Thomas had closed the theatre for the day as a mark of respect. The Campion's folk had done their best to find black mourning clothes. So much so that it was apparent several of them had raided the costume store. O'Leary was wearing a black cloak with a fur trim that Rosie recognised from the melodrama *Spring-heeled*

Jack, and Molly had decked herself out in a dress that had been used in the pantomime *Babes in the Wood*. Several others were wearing wraps and shawls purloined from the Campion's costume store to cover more flamboyant colours. Every now and then a dark shawl would slip and there would be a flash of vibrant red or orange as if the Campion's performers were exotic birds trying desperately to camouflage themselves. They weren't doing a very good job of it, thought Rose. She knew it would have made Ned laugh. Not that there was much else to laugh at today.

There were also some hall people who had worked with Ned in pantomime at the Shaftesbury, and some stagehands and performers from the Fortune in Shoreditch, but there was no family. Like Grace, Rose thought it likely that Ned was a runaway. She wondered whether there was a mother somewhere who left a light burning in the porch every night in case her son returned. Now he never would.

Rose spotted a man in the crowd she didn't know, standing slightly apart from the rest. He had a small waxed moustache and he was wearing a low crown bowler hat. There was something about the way he slouched disrespectfully against a weeping angel statue that made Rose confident he wasn't a mourner. So why was he here? She wondered whether he was a policeman. But he didn't look like a rozzer. He kept staring at Effie, who kept her eyes firmly lowered as if trying to avoid his gaze. Did they know each other?

Aurora was wondering about the man too. There was something familiar about him but she couldn't place him. She glanced at Rose, who gave her a wan little smile. Since the bicycle performance a few nights ago her life had improved immeasurably. Lizzie was so bereft at the theft of her box that she seemed to have quite lost interest in Aurora and was more or less leaving her to her own devices.

Lizzie had raged about her loss, and demanded the place be turned upside down. There had been a search but, as several people pointed out, leaving a snoozing O'Leary on the stage door was a bit like saying "Come on in!" to every Tom, Dick or Harry who happened to be passing. What with the workmen coming in and out, and the flower and laundry deliveries, anyone could have passed through Campion's that afternoon, taking Lizzie's box with them.

It served Lizzie right for not keeping her trunk locked.

Thomas had complete faith in the Campion's performers and backstage staff – who all knew that stealing would never be tolerated. When Thomas proposed that they call the police, Lizzie had seemed as opposed to the idea as she was to telling anyone exactly what was in the box. She had merely just kept muttering, "My treasure. Priceless. Irreplaceable."

"And probably stolen too," Rose had observed. Aurora wondered if Rose was right. Why would Lizzie have a silver cup belonging to the Easingford family? Was she trying to blackmail them in some way as she had other people? She remembered the envelope she had glimpsed in the hansom cab, the one addressed to a residence in Silver Square. Could it be the home of the Easingford family? She glanced around the crowd. Her eyes came to rest on Lottie. She looked more closely. She was sure that Lottie was wearing her shawl, the one that the laundry swore blind they had returned but which Aurora couldn't find. She didn't mind one bit. She just wished that Lottie had asked.

The service was drawing to an end. The

gravedigger lifted the first clod of earth on to the coffin. Grace and Freddie stepped forward, reached into their pockets and pulled out some brightly coloured pieces of paper. They threw them over the grave and as the wind caught some of them it was apparent that they were shaped like butterflies, fluttering brightly before they fell and covering the top of the coffin so its surface danced with colour.

As the mourners started to walk down the church path, Rose heard the man with the moustache muttering, "Butterflies, eh? Well, well, well," to himself. He smiled as if something important had just fallen into place. She turned to make sure that she got a long, hard look at his face. As she did so, she saw a ghostly figure standing behind a gravestone. It was Ned. He looked straight at her and nodded as if encouraging her on. Then he simply disappeared. She looked around quickly to see if anyone else had spotted him.

"Are you all right, Rosie?" asked Thomas. "You look as if you've seen a ghost."

19

Thomas was doing the accounts. Audiences at Campion's had been up over the last week. Crowds had been queuing to see Rose and Aurora's bicycle act. The girls had been working hard on it and it was a winner.

Income was up, but Thomas's costs were up too. Lizzie Gawkin was milking him for everything she could get, saying she had to take into account her losses as a result of the theft, and the fact that she had been about to sign a very lucrative contract for Aurora at the Blackfriars. Thomas might have told Lizzie to stuff her demands, as he could easily have found somebody else to do the bicycle act with Rose, but the thought of poor Aurora being turned into a spectacle at the Blackfriars – one of London's rowdiest dens of iniquity – was too much for Thomas's kind heart to bear. Besides, she and Rose seemed to be striking up a friendship now that Lizzie was less in evidence. Aurora had even left her lodging house and moved into Campion's for a few days, sharing top to tail in the bed with Rose.

There were other costs too. He intended to look after Grace and Freddie, and had found a little house for them just round the corner. They were going to move in later today. He glanced out of the window and saw Grace and the boy stepping into a carriage. They were briefly returning to Shoreditch to collect the last of their meagre possessions, although Grace hadn't even been sure there'd be anything left to collect.

He'd offered to accompany them but Grace had declined. Thomas respected her decision, suspecting that she didn't want him to see the circumstances in which the little family had been living. Thomas hated London's slum landlords, often rich, landed gentry who lived far away in splendour on their fine estates, while their tenants existed in squalor in run-down housing that was a danger to their health.

The carriage containing Grace and Freddie

set off and Thomas returned to his columns of figures, determined that it would be the last trip to the slums they'd ever have to make.

* ✳ *

Rose and Aurora were on the stage in the empty theatre rehearsing their act. Effie was sitting in the auditorium watching while she mended some of the ballet girls' costumes. The girls completed a circuit on the bicycle and jumped off laughing. Rose suddenly had an idea.

"What if you dressed as a boy? It would give the act a more daring edge. The crowd would go wild for it," said Rose. "You'd make such a beautiful boy, Aurora."

"Not as beautiful as the girl Freddie makes when Lottie and the other girls dress him up. When he dances the cancan with them between shows, nobody would ever know he was a boy."

"I know. They even call him Dora!" said Rose. "He's so sweet, and he loves it. He's a performer through and through, like Ned was. I wonder whether Grace would allow him to do it on stage. I used to dance alongside the girls when I was a tot and it was very popular."

Lottie, who had offered to cast a critical eye

over Rose and Aurora's act, arrived in the auditorium just in time to hear the end of their conversation.

"Gracie don't mind. I asked her before they went to Shoreditch," she said.

"Did they go on their own?" asked Rose sharply. The stranger at the funeral had unsettled her.

Lottie nodded. "Thomas offered to go but Grace wasn't 'aving it."

"It ain't a nice place," said Effie. "Full of lowlife."

"Effie," said Rose, "who was that man at the funeral, the one with the low crown bowler and the moustache like a slug? He looked at you as if he knew you."

Effie blushed. "Nah, I don't know him from Adam."

"Who's Adam?" chorused Aurora and Lottie together, and they fell about laughing. Rose laughed too, but she was certain that Effie was lying.

* ✳ *

Lizzie sat up in bed with a jug of gin by her side and considered how to make the best of the situation. After the theft of the box, she had raged and wailed. All her patience had come to naught.

It felt as if everything had gone wrong as soon as she'd set foot back in Southwark. She couldn't believe her eyes when, coming out of the post office on that first morning, she had run into the very last man on earth that she expected to see. She'd know that open, handsome face anywhere. How could she ever forget it, or the look of trust on his face when he had tenderly handed over his tiny baby daughter to her and implored Lizzie to keep her safe until he could return to fetch her. He'd barely looked a day older than he had on that day, almost thirteen years ago now, though his face then had been etched with grief for his wife, Louisa, who had died from fever after giving birth.

Lizzie had come across him in the street all those years ago, holding the baby and weeping. She'd hoped to pick his pocket but he'd clutched her arm and told her his desperate story. As soon as she set eyes on the silver cup with the blue ribbon tied to the handle that the desperate young man was offering to give her, Lizzie had seen her opportunity.

She told him to come and see her later at the

Victorious. When he did, she had assured him in her most motherly tones that his little baby would be in the safest possible hands with her, an experienced nanny. She showed him a number of references from satisfied parents that she had forged herself, and also the other little newborn that she was looking after temporarily for a friend in need. Well, that was her story. In fact, she had filched the child out of a pram by the Haymarket stage door only that morning, intending to strip the mewling little thing of its clothes and flog them as soon as it was safe and she could dump the babe in the river. She had even slipped her friend Eliza a few bob to come and assure young Edward that Lizzie had looked after her sister's babe and even saved his life when he had gone down with the measles. Eliza Chowser didn't have a sister.

The young man said he had nothing else to his name but the cup, and if she would take it temporarily, along with his daughter, when he returned from his tour of the provinces playing Ferdinand in *The Tempest* he would be able to pay her what he owed her for caring for the babe and reclaim his daughter and cup. The poor fool. He clearly had no idea of the value of the silver cup. Solid silver. He could tour the provinces for a year and still not have earned anywhere near its value.

Lizzie had asked how he came by it. Edward said his dad Joe, who was originally from Yorkshire, had told him it had been given to him and his wife, Abigail, in return for good service, and that it wasn't worth much, but that Joe held it in great sentimental value. He had told Edward that the boy should always keep it because it connected him with Yorkshire, where he had been born.

Lizzie thought this was an unlikely story. The gentry didn't hand out silver cups for good service. This Joe and Abigail had obviously prigged it and left Yorkshire in a hurry.

And then came that nasty business with the tenor, and she'd had to dump the babies and flee to her sister's. That's where she heard another version of the story – a version that she knew would make her fortune. She also realised what a mistake she'd made in getting rid of that baby. It was only lucky that she hadn't thrown the infants in the river as she'd intended, and just dumped them on a music-hall step instead. The cup plus the ribbon plus

Edward's child were blackmailer's gold.

So she had returned to Campion's to retrieve the baby. Only, when she had looked down at the two infants in their cribs she'd no idea which one was which. She had stood there dithering, when she realised she'd been spotted. She had picked up both babies and fled, but she'd had to drop one again or risk being caught.

Coming back to the scene of the crime with the Infant Phenomenon risked discovery, of course. Thomas Campion only had to realise she was the woman he had spotted that day and she'd be in big trouble. But running into Edward outside the post office was even more alarming. She had been so confident that he was far, far away. If he recognised her, all would be lost. Instead of milking Lord Easingford for every penny she could get, she would end up behind bars for child abduction, maybe worse. The young man had to go. It was his fault for being in the wrong place at the wrong time. In some ways, killing him had just been self-defence.

Lizzie took a slug of gin and continued to think things through. And now, after everything, someone had taken the box containing the cup and ribbon. At first she'd been quite certain that Snetherbridge had had a hand in its disappearance. She'd been furious at the thought of the lawyer and Lord Henry laughing at how they'd got one over on Lizzie Gawkin. But who was to say that someone from Campion's hadn't prigged the box? They were a bunch of lowlife thieves and vagabonds, every one of them. Whoever took it probably just slung the papers in the river and flogged the silver cup first chance they got.

It made her task harder, but she still knew what she knew. Nobody could take that away from her. And knowledge was power. She'd just have to bluff it out.

She determined to write to Mr Snetherbridge again. She would be elegantly restrained, and test the lie of the land. If he didn't reply, she would know they had the box. If he did, then she might still be able to squeeze something out of them if she was clever. Perhaps if she told them how she'd murdered Edward, they'd realise how far she'd go to protect the interests of the Easingford family. She had made quite sure that Lord Henry's nephew couldn't make things difficult for him and he should be grateful to her. She just had to make him see it that way.

* ✳ *

Rose found O'Leary sitting outside the theatre, wrapped up against the cold and guarding the stage door. He put a leg out to stop her passing.

"What's this?" she laughed.

"I'm redeeming myself, Rosie. I've not touched a drop of the gin before noon since the afternoon of the robbery. I'm like a guard dog here; I'm not letting anyone in or out unless I knows them."

"But you *do* know me, so you can let me out," said Rose.

O'Leary nodded. "Oh, I know you all right. And I knows Thomas, who went out a few minutes past for his appointment with that bank of his that gives him so much grief. But I wouldn't let in the man with the waxed moustache."

Rose looked alert. She was certain she knew who O'Leary meant.

"Was he wearing a low crown bowler hat?"

"Yes," said O'Leary, looking surprised.

"What did he want?" asked Rose.

"He said he wanted to talk to little Effie."

"Did he now…" said Rose.

"Yes," said O'Leary. "I told him he would have to make an appointment. He wouldn't get in without one. Not with me on the door." The old man looked pleased with himself. "In fact, it wasn't his lucky day. He wanted to see Grace and little Freddie too, but I told him he couldn't because they'd gone to Shoreditch."

"Did you tell him where?" asked Rose urgently.

O'Leary shook his head. "Didn't need to. He said he already knew where they lived."

Rose turned and ran back into the theatre and found Aurora. "There you are!" she cried. "Quick! We've got to go to Shoreditch. I've a feeling that Grace and Freddie are in terrible danger."

20

As they headed over London Bridge, Rose told Aurora that she thought the man with the slug-like moustache might have something to do with Ned's death.

"Some might say you're being fanciful, Rose, but now you say it, I know I have seen him before at the Four Cripples. He comes and sits at the next table when Lizzie is drinking."

Rose frowned. What was the man's interest in Lizzie? "Maybe he's trying to overhear your conversation," she said.

"It's never a conversation," said Aurora, tart as a plum.

Just then Rose gave a low whistle and pulled Aurora back. "Look!" she breathed, pointing down a narrow passageway. Effie was standing with the very man they were discussing. They were shouting at each other. At that moment, a woman turned down the passageway and Josiah stalked off quickly, leaving Effie staring after him.

"I know this sounds awful, and I don't even want to think it," said Rose. "But do you think Effie might be involved? Given that she knows that bloke?"

"Effie?" said Aurora. "Murder? Don't be daft, Rosie. You've taken two and two and made at least seven. There could be any number of reasons why that man's been hanging around. Maybe it's Effie he's really interested in, and not Grace and Freddie at all. Maybe she's the one who needs protection. Maybe we're off on a wild-goose chase to Shoreditch to help two people who don't need help at all, when it's Effie who needs looking after."

"Then why did he ask O'Leary about Grace and Freddie?"

"I don't know," said Aurora. "But I really don't have Effie down as an accessory to murder. *If* Ned was even murdered! We don't even know that, and we certainly have no proof that man was involved, let alone poor little Effie."

Rose started walking very quickly with her eyes fixed ahead. Aurora knew that she had upset her but she'd begun to think that she shouldn't have listened to Rose's hunch. Grace and Freddie were probably already in a hansom cab on their way back to Campion's.

* ✻ *

As soon as they entered the network of narrow streets behind the Bethnal Green Road it felt as if they were in a fiendishly difficult maze. As they plunged further in, the rumble of the traffic from the road grew muffled until they could hardly hear it at all. Rose walked ahead, and Aurora feared that if she let her out of her sight Rose would disappear into one of the passageways and vanish forever.

They picked their way through the Shoreditch streets, stepping over piles of rubbish as they went. People watched them pass, curious about these unknown children walking deep into the labyrinth of courtyards and narrow passageways. Dogs yapped at their ankles and chased chickens out of their way. Down one dark alleyway Rose even thought she glimpsed a pig. A few bare-footed urchins ran after them, begging for money. Some disappeared down secret alleys and then reappeared unexpectedly a few steps in front of them. Aurora sighed and just hoped she and Rose wouldn't get hopelessly lost.

Rose turned another corner and led them into a narrow street. "It's number one hundred and five," she said shortly.

They stopped outside a run-down house. It was in far better condition than the tumbledown dwellings on the other side of the street, many of which had missing doors and no glass. Rose rapped on the door. "Grace!" she called.

There was no reply. Rose tried the door handle. It turned and she pushed the door open. The bare room in front of them was damp but scrupulously clean. There was no sign of Grace and Freddie. The room, thought Rose, was filled with a melancholy emptiness as if their absence was as tangible a thing as a chair or a table. It made her feel more concerned than ever.

Aurora looked at her pensive face. "I'll ask down the street, see if anyone has seen them," she said, and disappeared out of the door.

Rose knew that Aurora was humouring her. She thought Rose had brought them on a wild goose chase and at this very moment Grace and

Freddie were probably sitting with Thomas in their new house having tea and crumpets. But what if they weren't? Her unease at the empty room was growing, not dissipating. She eyed the room for clues, trying to study it in the way that the police might look at the scene of a crime. She noticed one of the bricks at the bottom of the fireplace was wonky and loose. She bent down and tried to pull at it. When it wouldn't budge, she pulled a hairpin from her pocket and slid it down the side of the brick. She applied pressure and eased it forward. The brick shifted very slightly. She tried again and this time managed to move it forward far enough so that her fingers could grip it. It slid out with only a little resistance.

At the back of the small dark cavity where the brick had been, Rose saw a flash of white. She reached in, wary in case a mouse or worse was living there and nipped her fingers. She felt something. She pulled and it came away. It was an old envelope, dusty and streaked with mud. The envelope was empty but it was addressed to Ned and postmarked just before Christmas, around the same time that the Dorsets had first returned to London. She turned the envelope over. There was a return address: The Reverend Oliver Dorset Woldingham, The Parsonage, Easingford, Yorks.

There were also two lines scrawled in what Rose recognised as Ned's distinctively untidy hand:

Bess Jingle, Eliza Chowser, the Victorious.

Rose started because of what was written on the second line:

Campion's, Rose and ?

Why was her name there? And who or what did the question mark stand for? Aurora burst back through the door, so she stuffed it into her pocket for safe-keeping.

"Good news, Rosie!" she said. "I spoke to a neighbour. Grace took some stuff round that she didn't want to take with her, and both she and Freddie are fine. We've only just missed them. This neighbour said she'll show us the quickest way to the Bethnal Green Road where they were headed to pick up a hansom. Thought we might even catch them if we hurry."

The woman was as good as her word, leading them expertly through the narrow alleys and pointing them towards an archway that led out on to the Bethnal Green Road. The children ran gratefully towards the light, pleased to be out of the dingy, depressing maze of streets. Immediately they hit a wall of noise. The street was thronged with people and hawkers all shouting and calling. The cabs rolling across the cobbles sounded like large animals growling. A blind fiddler stood in the corner recreating the sound of farmyard animals with his bow, while further down the road a woman was playing a cornet extremely badly.

"Look, there they are!" shouted Aurora over the din, pointing across the road to where Grace was holding Freddie's hand and looking for an empty hansom. "All safe and well; nothing to worry about."

The girls went to cross the road to catch up with them but the carts and cabs were thick and they had to wait. They saw Grace turn down a quieter side street, walking quickly. Rose guessed she was cutting through to the next main street in the hope it would be easier to pick up a cab. A rather fancy carriage with a crest on its side, entwining an 'I' and an 'H' in a flowery motif, turned down the narrow street after Grace and Freddie.

There was a sudden gap in the vehicles on

the main road and the children darted into the middle, then waited while another cart rumbled by before making it to the other side. They turned right down the side street where Grace and Freddie had gone. They could see that the fancy carriage had stopped up ahead with its door open, just a little way in front of Grace and Freddie. A man – brawny and squat like a toad – stepped out in front of Grace. The children saw her take a step backwards, and she shouted, "Run, Freddie!" as the man seized her by the arms. Freddie stood frozen with shock, while Grace shouted again for him to run. But it was too late because at that moment the man with the slug-like moustache and low crown bowler appeared from around the other side of the coach and grabbed him.

The children raced towards Grace as she was manhandled towards the carriage door. She was protesting loudly, but the street was almost deserted and nobody helped.

Rose launched herself like a small steam train at the man who was pushing Grace into the carriage. Aurora came to her aid and was rewarded by being punched so hard in the stomach that her legs folded beneath her. Rose looked wildly around. Slug Face had Freddie in his arms, who was kicking and screaming.

"Aurora, help Freddie!" yelled Rose as she renewed her efforts to pull the man off Grace. But he was too strong for her, and he held a handkerchief over Grace's mouth and nose as he forced her into the coach. Rose caught a whiff of chloroform and Grace went limp.

The man snapped down the blinds. Rose beat her fists helplessly on the glass. Slug Face had Freddie by his arms and a hand over his mouth. Aurora was hitting and kicking the man, who was trying to push her away.

Rose turned and stormed Slug Face, slamming her body into him as hard as she could. His elbow caught her on the nose and she reeled in pain. But she wouldn't be beaten. She moved around to his front and dealt him a sharp kick on the shin that made him loosen his grip on Freddie. Rose grabbed Freddie by one arm and Aurora succeeded in landing a low punch in Slug Face's stomach. Rose began pulling Freddie away, but at that moment the carriage door opened and the other man jumped out, throwing Aurora to the ground. Slug Face picked up Freddie and slung him over his shoulder while his accomplice pushed Rose so hard that she reeled into the display of cabbages outside a shop, sending them flying. The battle was lost.

But before Slug Face reached the carriage door, there was a furious battle cry. Effie – a pedalling Boudicca on a green bicycle covered with daisies – ploughed straight into the men at top speed, scattering them like skittles at a country fair. Aurora grabbed Freddie by the arm and ran with him up the street. Rose leapt into the coach to try and rouse Grace as Effie spun round on the bicycle and pedalled furiously back towards the two men, once again intent on a head-on collision with them.

"You'll pay for this, Effie. I'll see you hanged by the neck before I'm done," shouted Josiah as she careered into him and the bike skittered into the road, sending Effie sprawling. He nodded curtly to the other man. "Get on your way with the woman; I'll find the kid and deal with him."

The men hurried into the coach, hauled Rose out of it and flung her to the ground like a piece of rubbish. The coachman flicked his whip and the horses set off at a gallop, only narrowly avoiding Effie. Slug Face melted away into an alleyway. Rose, bruised and battered, pulled herself painfully to her feet and went over to help Effie up, but she shrugged her away.

"Leave me, I'm fine. Go after Aurora and Freddie. They'll need your help if Josiah Pinch is after them."

"So you do know that man, Effie," said Rose sharply.

"Yes," whispered Effie. "I lied to you."

Rose stared at her for a second, then she turned and ran in the direction the others had taken. Effie looked sadly after her. She had seen the look of mistrust mingled with disgust on Rose's face. She knew she could never return to Campion's. Not now. They would all know that she wasn't to be trusted.

Rose, Aurora and Freddie crouched in an alleyway off a small side street and tried to catch their breath. Freddie was crying softly. The two girls tried to soothe him.

"Why have those men taken my mum?" he asked.

Rose hugged him. "We're going to find out, and we're going to get your mum back."

"Now?" asked Freddie hopefully.

"First we need to get you safely back to Campion's." She turned to Aurora. "Did you see the crest on the side of that carriage? It might help us find out where Grace has been taken."

"I did," said Aurora, "and I've seen it before."

"Where?"

"On a piece of notepaper in Lizzie's box,

the one that was stolen. It stands for Ivanhoe House." Aurora looked at Freddie and gave Rose a warning glance. Then she mouthed silently over his head, "It's an asylum for the insane. In Balham."

Rose gasped. The idea of Grace being forcibly taken to a mental asylum was horrifying. "We've got to get back to Campion's, and fast. Come on."

They peered out of the alleyway. She was sure Josiah Pinch would give up looking for them in Shoreditch and concentrate on catching them as they closed in on Campion's. She looked down at Freddie's tear-streaked face. He was exhausted and drowsy in her arms. How were they going to get into Campion's without being caught?

"Do you have a plan, Rose?" asked Aurora. Rose shook her head hopelessly.

"Maybe we should look for Effie…" Aurora trailed off, seeing Rose's face.

"I know she helped us just now but she lied about knowing that man. He's called Josiah Pinch, and until we know what's going on, I don't know if we can trust her." Rose frowned as a plan formed in her mind.

"That's it!" she said. "We'll go to the Fortune;

it's not far from here. They'll help us. Hall folk always help other hall people. We can get them to send a message to Thomas."

* ✳ *

A cloud of face powder billowed up in the dressing room and made Rose sneeze. Tilly Tiptree, known as "the Fortune's Jewel", was a singer whose rich voice carried above even the noisiest audience and whose quick wits and improvised repartee could quell any heckler. She put down the powder puff and stepped back to admire her handiwork.

"There! You'd never guess he was a boy," she said, taking a piece of burnt cork and darkening Freddie's lashes.

"Wish I had lashes like yours, Freddie lad," said Tilly. "You're a real little beaut. Give us a twirl."

Freddie scrambled down from the stool and turned in his petticoats, trying to do high kicks as he twirled. Tilly laughed and gave him a boiled sweet. She turned to Rose and Aurora.

"What do you think? Even his own granny wouldn't recognise him, would she, if it wasn't for that little butterfly birthmark on his neck?"

"You've done a wonderful job, Tilly," said

Rose. "We can't thank you enough."

"Glad to be of help," said Tilly, then she cast a critical eye over Aurora and tucked an escaping curl back under her cap.

"You make a very good boy, an' all. That little suit is a perfect fit. You just need to make sure that your hair stays up under your cap." She added, "I'm going to give this brave little chap a cake before you set off," and she led Freddie away. They could hear her reminding him that he was only to answer to the name Dora.

"Right," said Rose, turning to Aurora. "Let's run over the plan again. I'm getting a hansom all the way back to Campion's, but I'm going to drop you and Freddie off in a quiet side street a little way before the bridge. Then you two will saunter over the bridge and down to the mudlarks. If Josiah's on the bridge, he'll be looking for two girls and a small boy. Or a girl and a small boy, but not the other way round. I'm certain you could walk right under his nose and he'd never know."

"You sure we shouldn't wait until Thomas returns from his meetings?" asked Aurora anxiously. "Wouldn't it be safer if he just came to get us?"

Rose shook her head. "Lottie sent back a message saying Thomas might be out until this evening. It could be hours before he gets here, hours during which something terrible could be happening to Grace."

* ✳ *

Rose took a cab all the way back to Campion's, as planned. She found that Thomas had just returned and was beside himself with worry over the original message she had sent from the Fortune. He'd been about to set off there but when Rose told Thomas her plan, he immediately rushed off to see his lawyer, Mr Cherryble, about Grace's abduction.

"If she's in Ivanhoe House I won't rest until I've got her released," said Thomas, pulling on his coat. "Don't you fret, Rosie."

As soon as Thomas left, Rose went downstairs to find Lottie, Molly and Tess and explain what they needed to do.

* ✳ *

Aurora walked slowly over London Bridge, holding tightly to Freddie's hot little hand. They were so close to Campion's but so far away too. The urge to run home was a strong one. But Rose had given her strict instructions that she was to look as if she had all the time in the world. Aurora even stopped in the middle of the bridge to point out the great dome of St Paul's to Freddie, as if they were just enjoying a relaxing tour of the sights.

The two of them had nearly crossed the bridge. Aurora was certain everyone was looking at them curiously and that they would shortly be exposed. She passed the sheet-music sellers and a troupe of acrobatic dwarfs, and the food sellers all shouting themselves hoarse trying to sell hot eels and pea soup. She tried hard not to scan the faces of those loitering at the end of the bridge, although when a sallow man, as tall and thin as a ladder, started walking towards them her heart only stopped hammering when she realised he was greeting a woman walking directly behind them. A gaggle of men seemed to be looking for someone in the crowd coming towards them, but they didn't give Aurora and Freddie a second glance. There was no sign of Josiah Pinch.

She turned left at the end of the bridge and walked along the side of the river. In the distance she could see Lottie and a whole crowd of the ballet girls down on the muddy shore with the grimy mudlarks gathered around them, jumping and shouting. The mudlark children loved the hall performers, who never stuck their noses up at them. As they came closer, she saw that Lottie and the others were distributing ginger beer and Chelsea buns.

Aurora glanced around and then sat down on a bench. She could see no sign of anyone watching them. She got Freddie to slip his feet out of his boots and then she whispered in his ear, "See, Freddie, it's Lottie and the other girls, with the mudlarks. Run down to her and she'll have a bun for you and then she'll take you back to Campion's to see Rose." She gave him a little push, and for a second he looked trustingly in her eyes, then he ran down the riverbank, his tattered petticoats flapping, and was soon swallowed up in the middle of the other children. A few minutes later Lottie and the ballet girls began shepherding the children towards Campion's, where they had all been promised their own little show.

* ✳ *

Rose peeped from Thomas's study window, making sure she was standing well back so as not to be spotted by Josiah, who was lurking by the yard gate.

She held her breath as Lottie and the other girls strolled up Hangman's Alley with the gaggle of mudlark children. She watched Josiah suddenly stand up straighter. She saw him step forward, the better to scan all the boys' faces closely. She held her breath, then sighed with relief as he returned to his pipe, an air of disappointment apparent in the slump in his shoulders. None of the boys were Freddie.

The children disappeared through Campion's stage door, chattering excitedly to each other as Rose went to greet them and scooped Freddie up in her arms. "You did well, little Dora," she whispered.

Half an hour later she let the mudlarks out of the door and watched as they sped off past Josiah down towards the river, shouting and laughing. The man didn't even bother to look up as a serious-looking boy of about thirteen sauntered slowly across the yard. The boy held the door of Campion's open as Lizzie Gawkin swept out with barely a glance at the child. The boy disappeared into the theatre.

"Aurora!" cried Rose, and she enveloped her in a bear hug. "You did it!"

Aurora grinned. "Even Lizzie didn't recognise me. Lottie did bring Freddie in, didn't she?" she asked.

"Yes," said Rose. "It all worked beautifully. Josiah didn't even give Freddie or you a second glance. It just goes to show that people only see what they expect to see. They often can't see the truth even when it's staring them right in the face."

22

It was very late. Downstairs the staff were clearing up from the evening performances. Occasionally somebody could be heard calling goodnight as they went home. But the lamp in Thomas's window burned bright.

Freddie was asleep in the next room, exhausted by the day's events. Thomas, Rose and Aurora were holding a war council.

"Dr Fogg, the director of Ivanhoe House, denies all knowledge of Grace," said Thomas. "My lawyer went to Balham to meet him and he was quite insistent that no patients have been admitted today. Mr Cherryble, a sound judge of character, is convinced that Dr Fogg is lying but could hardly accuse him to his face. It wouldn't help us, in any case. But he did see one of the carriages and drew the crest." He showed the paper to the children.

"That's it," said Rose. "No doubt about it. It was on the carriage that took Grace away."

Thomas sighed. "Mr Cherryble says that if we have proof Grace is being held at the asylum against her will, he can start legal proceedings to get her out. But if they deny she's incarcerated and we have no proof that they're lying, there's nothing he can legally do." Everyone looked horrified, and Thomas shook his head sorrowfully.

"The real question," said Rose, "is why does whoever took Grace want her and Freddie? Josiah Pinch must be working for somebody, somebody influential enough to have Dr Fogg in his pay. So why are they such a threat?"

"It's a mystery," said Thomas, "but it must be connected with poor Ned's death. I should have listened to you, Rosie." He frowned. "Maybe whoever snatched her is worried that Grace knows something about Ned's death. Maybe something that even she doesn't realise she knows. Some crucial clue."

"There's something else," said Rose, producing the envelope she found in the house in Shoreditch. "This connects Ned to a place called Easingford in Yorkshire and somebody named Oliver Dorset Woldingham."

"Oh!" exclaimed Aurora. "Easingford was the name on a silver cup that I found in Lizzie's box!"

"The box that disappeared?" asked Thomas. He'd gone over to his bookshelves and seemed to be looking for something.

Aurora nodded. "I didn't take it, but it was my fault it got stolen. I left Lizzie's trunk unlocked." She blushed. "I'd pilfered Lizzie keys while she was drunk so I could take a look. I wanted to see if there was anything about my past in there. That's where I saw the crest for Ivanhoe House too, and…" She paused.

"Go on," said Rose gently.

"There were some letters in the trunk that made me think Lizzie is a blackmailer. And that she's been doing it for years."

Rose was frowning again. "This is getting more and more confusing. We already know that Effie knew Grace from Shoreditch, and that she has some connection with that lowlife Josiah Pinch."

Thomas peered over his glasses. "Any news

of little Effie?"

Rose and Aurora shook their heads. Rose hoped that Effie was all right, but the fact she hadn't returned to Campion's fed her suspicions about the girl, whether she'd helped them escape from Josiah or not.

"Let's go over what we know," she suggested. "So, Lizzie Gawkin has some link with Easingford. So there's a possibility that Josiah, Effie and Lizzie could all be in league with each other.

"We also know from the envelope I discovered that Ned had a correspondence with the parson at Easingford, Oliver Dorset Woldingham. Given the 'Dorset' in his name, do you think that he could be Ned's father? And see here: there are some names written in Ned's hand on the envelope."

She pushed the envelope towards Aurora, who examined it and then looked up at Rose with a frown.

"Why's your name here?"

Rose shrugged. "I've no idea. I don't know who Bess Jingle or Eliza Chowser are either."

Thomas suddenly gave a little cry of triumph and came back to the table with a book in his hand. "Look at this," he said, pointing to one of the pages. "Easingford is a small village in Yorkshire that forms part of a big estate belonging to the Easingford family. They own everything for miles around, including a large house, Easingford Hall. The family crest is a butterfly. The family motto is *By all means necessary*. Henry Edgar Easingford is the current lord. He had a twin brother, older by a few minutes, called Frederick Edward Easingford who died thirty-two years ago. Aha! Listen to this – Frederick Easingford was married to a Lily Clara Dorset."

"Dorset!" said Rose. "Just like Ned, and the parson who wrote the letter."

Everyone looked very alert.

"But," continued Thomas, "they'd only been married for three months when he died."

"So his younger twin, Henry, inherited the title?" asked Aurora.

"Not immediately," said Thomas. "It seems Lily was pregnant when her husband died. Six months later she gave birth to a son, Edward Frederick Dorset Easingford. Looking at the dates here, both mother and son died on the day of the child's birth. If the child had survived, he would have been the current Lord Easingford. But instead, his uncle Henry inherited everything."

Thomas gave a little whistle, while everyone tried to absorb this information.

"Blow me if Henry doesn't then go and marry another Dorset girl, Sarah Charlotte." He ran his finger down the page. "She was Lily's younger sister and according to the dates she was barely seventeen when they got married. She had Lord Henry Easingford's only child a year later, a son named Edgar Easingford."

"It's all very interesting, but I don't see how this helps us," said Aurora. "Except that there must be some connection between Ned and the Dorset sisters and the parson, and if we could find out what it is it may help."

"It's all we have to go on. If only we could talk to Grace. She always said there was something mysterious about Ned's background. Maybe she just didn't think it was relevant to his death," said Rose. "Sometimes you can know something, but you just don't realise its significance."

"I'm going to write to Oliver Dorset Woldingham," said Thomas, "and hope that he can shed some light on the situation. In the meantime, we have to do our best to keep little Freddie safe and find out what has happened to his poor mother. I only wish I knew how we are ever going to get proof that she's locked up in Ivanhoe House."

"I know how we could!" said Rose suddenly, bobbing up and down in excitement. "You're going to hate the idea, Thomas, but you won't talk me out of it."

* ✳ *

Rose and Aurora waved goodbye to Lottie, Jem and the last stragglers who had been drinking after the show. Rose heard Jem trying to persuade Lottie to lend him sixpence for a tip he had for a big horse race tomorrow. Their voices faded, and Rose eased the bolt across the Campion's door. They had twice been round the building to check that every door and window was secure. O'Leary was already snoring under the stage where he always slept. The children were about to go upstairs when Rose put a finger to her lips. "I think I heard something outside," she whispered.

The girls listened hard. The gate gave its distinctive squeak. Rose picked up a chair and held it over her head while Aurora pulled the newly oiled bolt back silently. Aurora flung the door open and the girls came face to face with Effie. Startled, Rose dropped the chair she was holding with a crash. "Just bringing your bicycle back," Effie whispered.

"Are you all right?" Aurora asked her.

Effie glanced at Rose. "I owe you an explanation."

"You do," said Rose with a touch of chill in her voice. She saw Effie flinch and she thawed. "But we also owe you for helping to save Freddie. You'd better come in."

Effie crept into Campion's and Aurora secured the door again, after first sticking her head out into the yard to check Effie was alone. The children settled in the ballet girls' dressing room, and Rose got straight down to business.

"So," she said sternly. "How do you know Josiah Pinch?"

"He used to work for the rent collector over Shoreditch way. He put the frighteners on me mum and me when we fell behind with the rent."

"Shoreditch!" said Rose. "So he could have known Ned and Grace?"

Effie frowned. "Maybe, but I don't think so.

It was Lizzie Gawkin he was asking about. He only got interested in them when I mentioned a man called Ned Dorset had been murdered recently."

Rose and Aurora looked at each other excitedly. The Dorset connection again!

"When he cornered me this morning," said Effie, "he was grilling me about Grace and Freddie. Got really angry when I said I didn't know no more about them. It's why I headed Shoreditch way on the bicycle. I heard Grace telling Thomas she was going to Shoreditch. I reckoned she and Freddie might need help."

Rose looked thoughtful. "Why was he so interested in Lizzie Gawkin?"

Effie shrugged. "Dunno, really. He asked me to get hold of a silver cup and blue ribbon that he said she had."

"And did you?"

Effie bit her lip. "Yes and no. I ... I ... stole the box from her trunk. It was easy; she'd left it open. Soon as I took it, I knew it was a mistake and I wanted to put it back, but before I got the chance Lizzie found it was gone. But I was going to, cross me heart."

"Did you give it to Josiah?"

"No."

"So have you still got it?" asked Rose urgently. She felt sure the box contained the answers to all their questions.

"I know where it is," said Effie. "I put it in the props room in the trunk with loads of panto stuff in it. I didn't think anyone would notice it there."

The children looked at each other and immediately rushed to the props room.

"That one," said Effie, pointing to the trunk with "Aladdin" stencilled on the top. They rummaged around inside but although there were several boxes covered in paste jewels, Lizzie's box was nowhere to be seen.

"Are you sure you put it in this trunk?" asked Rose sharply.

"Yes," said Effie helplessly. "I know it was that one. I put Aurora's shawl on top. I … I know I did." Her lip was trembling. "Somebody must have taken it." She looked up at their sceptical faces. They didn't believe her.

"Effie," said Aurora gently. "Please don't lie to us. It doesn't matter how bad the truth is as long as it is the truth."

"I am telling the truth!" cried Effie desperately.

"I wouldn't lie…" She trailed off, thinking about Josiah Pinch. "All right, I *am* a liar. A liar and a thief. But I promise I'm telling the truth now. I swear on my mum's life."

Rose raised an eyebrow. "I thought you said your mother was dead."

Effie looked at her despairingly. "She ain't dead," she whispered. "She's locked up in Holloway for stealing a pocket watch. Only she didn't steal it. I did it. It was my first job. We were behind with the rent again. Josiah Pinch decided it was time I did some prigging meself, not just act as a lookout, and I panicked. Me mum took the blame to save me. Josiah knows and he threatened to tell the magistrates she'd lied under oath if I didn't steal the cup and ribbon and anything else of Lizzie Gawkin's I could find. He'd do it too. He ain't got a heart. If he did peach, me mum would get more time for lying, and I'd go to Holloway too. It would kill me mum if I went in the clink. We were always poor but we were respectable until we fell behind with the rent and Josiah got us in his clutches."

"Couldn't you just have told the landlord what he was doing?" asked Rose.

"You're joking, ain't you? Lord Easingford's the worst of the lot. He don't care how he gets his money."

The children stared at each other.

"What did you say he was called?" asked Rose, not sure she could believe her ears.

"Lord Easingford," said Effie, looking at their astonished faces.

"Effie, I want to be sure you are telling us the truth. When you came south over the river, did Josiah send you here?" asked Rose.

"No, cross me heart, he didn't," said Effie. "I came to make a new start. At first I thought he must have followed me here. But I reckon it was just bad luck. He already had business at Campion's and once he saw me, he realised I could be useful to him."

"And that business seems to have something to do with Lizzie Gawkin and Lord Easingford, and we know that Ned has an Easingford link too." Rose's mind was whirring. "Do you think that Lizzie could be blackmailing the Easingford family in some way and that Josiah is involved too?" she asked.

"It's a possibility," said Aurora.

"I think it all comes back to Ned," said Rose

excitedly. "If we could just find out what his connection is with the Easingford family, maybe we could discover why he was murdered. It makes it all the more urgent that we talk to Grace."

She looked round to ask Effie something, but Effie had gone. They rushed into the yard. Effie was walking away down Hangman's Alley, a small solitary figure illuminated in the pale eerie glow of a street lamp.

"Effie!" called Rose. "Effie! Come back."

The small figure didn't turn but simply continued to glide away from them like a lonely ghost. The girls ran to catch up with her.

"Where are you going?" asked Rose.

"I only come back to bring the bicycle. I knew you needed it for your act. I didn't want you to think I'd stolen it. I can't stay at Campion's, not now you all know I'm a liar and thief and I put Josiah Pinch on to Grace and Freddie."

Rose frowned. "Of course you're going to stay at Campion's, Effie. You didn't know that by telling him about Ned you'd be putting Grace and Freddie in danger."

"It don't change the fact I'm a liar and a thief," said Effie in a tiny voice.

"Oh, Effie, you're also brave and loyal! Look at the way you put yourself in danger trying to save Freddie!" said Aurora.

Rose looked at Effie solemnly. "You must stay. We want you to. Campion's needs you, Effie!" Rose put her arm around Effie's thin shoulders and steered her back towards the theatre and inside. "And from what I can see, you need Campion's. It's obvious that you are just not cut out for a career in lying and thieving."

Effie smiled feebly. "I want to do everything I can to solve the mystery of Ned's death. There was something else Grace told me. She said that Ned told her he took his name off a gravestone. Later he said it was a joke. But I think she thought it was true."

Aurora, who was drawing the bolt across the door, suddenly gasped. "Easingford! I knew I'd seen that name somewhere else besides the cup. It's just come back. Lizzie had a newspaper cutting about Henry Easingford. It was something to do with him and the Queen. So there's definitely a connection between Lizzie and Lord Henry. Blackmail, most likely. She was always sending and receiving letters. She sent one the day we came here – I caught a glimpse of the address. It was going to Silver Square."

Rose turned and ran up the stairs to Thomas's study, beckoning the others after her, and opened the book that Thomas had shown them. She flicked through the pages and turned to the others. "Look! Lord Henry Easingford. London residence: 22 Silver Square."

The children looked at each other. They had lots of pieces of a puzzle, but no idea how they fitted together.

23

It was the next day, and Rose and Thomas were rattling along in a coach on their way to Ivanhoe House in Balham. Rose had persuaded Thomas to go along with her plan, even though he didn't like it one bit. He thought he was the one who needed his head examining for agreeing to it, but Rose could be very persuasive. The lawyer had told Thomas they needed proof that Grace was inside, so Rose was going to try and find her admissions form and pinch it, or, if that proved impossible, get Grace to sign a piece of headed notepaper saying she was being held against her will.

"Are you sure about this, Rose?" asked Thomas. "We could turn straight round and go back to Campion's, try to find another way to free Grace."

Rose shook her head firmly, her mouth set in a mutinous line. Thomas knew she wouldn't budge. The plan was for Thomas to pose as Mr Skimblebanks, the successful tea-merchant father of a wayward daughter, Sophia, who he wanted to tame. He would take her to the asylum and leave her there. Then, after twenty-four hours, Thomas would return, saying he had changed his mind and wished to have his daughter returned to him immediately. He would offer a handsome fee in return for the asylum's cooperation.

That gave Rose twenty-four hours to get some proof to take to a magistrate in order to secure Grace's release. Thomas wasn't at all happy about any of it, but at least he knew they both had the acting skills to carry it off. The girl sitting opposite him, wearing one of Campion's finest costumes, looked every inch the little lady.

Soon the narrow, muddy streets of Southwark gave way to broader avenues and hedges. There were snowdrops to be seen, and the odd goat. Hens pecked around the road.

"Thomas," said Rose quietly, "what would

happen if Campion's went under?"

"Don't you worry, Rosie, you and Aurora might just save the day with your bicycle act. But even if Campion's does fail, I'll look out for you. I might not be able to support every stray we've picked up at Campion's over the years, but I'd never abandon you."

"I'm not sure I could cope with being abandoned twice," said Rose in a little voice. Thomas glanced at her wan face. He knew that, secure though she was at Campion's, Rose found the fact she had been abandoned by her mother hard to accept.

"That's never going to happen, Rosie." Thomas turned quite pink. "I know I'm not your father, but I love you as if you were my own."

Rose took his hand and squeezed it tightly. She knew he was thinking of his own lost children, two little twin babes dead of the measles before their first birthday. Then she suddenly remembered something.

"Thomas?" she said tentatively, fearing she might be stepping into difficult territory. "I don't want to pry, but why was Ned asking you about your babies that day he and Grace came to tea?"

If she had suddenly held a knife to Thomas's neck, he couldn't have seemed more startled. A great struggle appeared to be taking place inside him.

"Not my babies, Rose," he said quietly. "*The* babies." He paused. "You and the other little one."

"What do you mean?" breathed Rose.

Thomas took a deep breath. "I don't know why I've never told you this before. You weren't the only child left on Campion's step that morning. There were two of you, both girls, both newborns."

"Two of us?" whispered Rose so quietly she could barely be heard. "I had a sister, a twin?"

Thomas shook his head. "I can't say you were twins, or even sisters. When I found you on the doorstep, it felt for a moment as if my own dear girls had come back to me. You were each wrapped in one half of the same linen sheet, and you looked alike just as all tiny babies do, with their blue eyes and downy hair. But as the days passed you looked far less alike to me and your colouring was very different, which made me think that maybe you weren't related at all."

"What happened to the other baby?"

Thomas looked upset. "Rosie, this isn't the time or the place to discuss it. Let's turn the carriage round and go home where we can talk properly. We'll come back to Ivanhoe House another day."

"No," said Rose, thrusting out her chin so she looked like a prize fighter. "We can't leave Grace, and I want to know. Now."

Thomas sighed and looked very sad. "All right then. It was about three weeks after I found you both at Campion's, and the pair of you were fast asleep, wrapped up in the baskets I'd bought for you both, out in the yard. O'Leary was doing a bit of scenery painting out there and keeping an eye on you. I was up in my study. He went inside to get some more paint, just as I happened to stand up and look down into the yard. There was a woman, thin and dark-haired, staring down into the baskets. I banged on the window, she looked up and I caught a glimpse of her face, and then she grabbed both baskets and rushed out of the yard. I ran after her. She was quick on her feet but burdened by the baskets. I had almost caught her when she suddenly dropped one of the baskets. It was the one with you in it.

"I bent to pick you up, and when I looked up she had disappeared down one of the narrow streets leading down to the river. Of course, I went after her. But there was no trace, so I reported what had happened to the police. But they had better things to investigate than another missing child."

"But she might have been my mother!" cried Rose. "It might have been my mother coming back for her two daughters. And I got left behind."

Thomas's face was flushed. "I told you, I don't think you and the other babe were sisters. And, Rose, don't you think that if she really was your mother, she would have knocked on the door and explained that she wanted you back? She'd have gone to the police if necessary, surely."

Rose knew that what Thomas was saying made sense but she still felt devastated. Maybe her mother had come back for her and Thomas had thwarted her. Maybe she hadn't just lost a mother but a sister too.

Tears were falling down her face. Thomas leaned forward and clasped her hands but Rose snatched them away. "Maybe she was my mother and now I'll never know her. I can't

215

believe you didn't tell me."

"I know I should have done," said Thomas sadly. "I wasn't trying to keep it a secret. There just never seemed the right moment to tell you. And I was so full of guilt and regret. I hadn't been able to protect my own children and I lost them, and then I had been given a second chance, a gift of two babes and I hadn't been able to protect them either, not properly. Whenever I think of that time I'm eaten up with loss and grief. So I tried not to think about it and I justified it to myself by saying what good would it do you knowing what happened. It would only make you unhappy."

"Well, it has," said Rose furiously, and then the words were out of her mouth and she couldn't take them back: "You had no right, you're not my real father."

"Oh, Rose, Rose," said Thomas ruefully. "I know that. You've brought me more—"

But Rose, consumed by her own misery, turned her face against him and before he could finish his sentence, the cab pulled into a wide drive and came to a standstill.

"We're 'ere, guv," said the coachman. Rose and Thomas stared out of the window at the

Georgian house in front of them. It was a grey, ivy-clad building with wide steps leading up to the door. It would have been rather pleasant if it were not for the thick iron bars on all the windows.

24

Rose lay awake in the narrow bed watching the moonlight spill through the bars of the window. She could see bodies hunched under blankets in other beds. She was regretting her final moments with Thomas before the door of Ivanhoe House had clanged behind him. He had been so desperate for her forgiveness, but she had turned away from him. When he had tried to kiss her goodbye she had pulled away.

"Goodbye, Mr Skimblebanks," said Dr Fogg, standing up behind his desk in the study and moving round to Thomas and pressing his hand. He started to guide Thomas towards the door. Seizing her chance, Rose leaned forward and grabbed a sheet of headed notepaper.

Dr Fogg was too busy trying to ease Thomas out of the study door to notice as Rose folded it swiftly and stuffed it up her knickerbockers. "I can assure you that you are leaving Sophia in the safest of hands. I am certain that you will notice a pleasing difference in her behaviour when you next see her." He glanced back at Rose standing behind them, her face all innocence, and determined to break this rich, spoiled, wayward girl.

"I shall come and visit my daughter often," said Thomas. They had reached the hall with its tiled black-and-white chequered floor. Two nurses appeared and flanked Rose, a little too close for comfort.

Dr Fogg's meaty lips stretched themselves into an oily smile.

"We do not recommend any contact for the first three months. We find that patients settle better without too much of a reminder of their old way of life."

Thomas raised an eyebrow. "Sophia is my daughter and I am paying for her stay here. Paying generously, I might add. I shall come and see her whenever I so desire."

"As you wish, sir," said Dr Fogg tightly.

At the door, Thomas turned to Rose. "It won't be for long, Sophia, I promise. I shall come by tomorrow before noon and check that all is well and you have settled."

Rose said nothing. She was no longer sure if she was acting or simply projecting her real feelings. Thomas stepped out into sunshine and she saw his shadow through the glass panels in the door, walking away from her.

Dr Fogg turned to the two nurses. They grabbed Rose by the arms.

"You will have to go easy on this one," he said curtly, "until her father loses interest in her." He put his face close to Rose and said silkily, "They do lose interest, you know, Sophia. We have had people here for years, girls just like you whose fathers or husbands find them too much to handle. They give them over to us and after a while it just seems to slip their minds that they left them here. It's so much more convenient for everyone that way."

Now, lying in the moonlight as she waited for the house to fall silent so that she could look for Grace, Rose regretted that she hadn't given Thomas a little sign that she had forgiven him and shown him how much she loved him.

She sat up in bed and listened. The moans and coughs had finally died away. Even the nurse at the end of the ward was snoring, her cap slipped across her eyes. She must find Grace. There had been no sign of her all day. But at supper she'd been given a clue when she'd overheard a conversation between two of the maids.

"I've got to climb those bloomin' stairs all the way to the third floor with a tray again," grumbled one. "That new one that was brought in screaming and kicking yesterday ain't settling. Me poor legs will suffer for it. We need 'elp. They've 'ad that notice for a new maid on the back door for ages and nobody has answered it. Nobody wants to work in a mad 'ouse. I'm rushed off me feet."

Rose hardly felt the cold linoleum as she stealthily crossed the room. Downstairs, beyond the imposing hall with its black-and-white tiles, Ivanhoe House was plush and carpeted, but away from any of the rooms that visitors might see, all expense had been spared.

Rose crept like a cat across the floor. She turned the handle of the ward door and it opened. She was not surprised. Everyone was so docile here there was no need to lock them in at night. She suspected most were being given laudanum. She checked the corridor and then padded upstairs. She heard a shriek and froze, before realising that it was only a fox outside. She tried a door, but the bed in the room was empty. She heard a noise at the end of the corridor and stayed in the empty room.

Two nurses walked by, talking. "That new one, Grace, is another of Easingford's relatives, just like old Sarah who's been here forever."

Rose suppressed a gasp. Sarah? Wasn't that the name of the younger Dorset sister?

Could it be that Sarah Easingford, Henry's wife, was an inmate too?

Rose waited until the voices faded. Then she tiptoed along the corridor and opened the door at the end. A shaft of moonlight fell on the iron bedstead and the figure strapped to the bed with leather belts. Grace turned her head and looked at Rose, her eyes dark with fear.

"Rose," she whispered. "Have they got you too? Oh, Rose, Rose. We are going to rot in here and die, and nobody will ever know." Her eyes darkened further. "Freddie?"

"He's safe and we're not going to rot and

die," said Rose firmly. "I'm here to get you out. Thomas is coming back for me tomorrow, and we'll get you released as quickly as we can. I promise you, Grace."

She produced the headed notepaper and a pencil from her knickerbockers, undid the straps and made Grace sign the short note she'd written earlier.

"Grace, did Ned ever mention somebody called Lord Easingford?" she said as she retied the straps.

Grace looked puzzled, but then she said, "No, but there was a funny thing happened in Oxford one night after the show. This real posh type seemed to think he knew Ned. Called him Easingford – Ed Easingford. He got quite nasty when Ned said he was mistaken. Shouted something about Ned being barmy and that it ran in the family. Afterwards Ned said the man must have mistaken him for someone else. But I could see he was rattled."

"That's—" began Rose. The fox screamed outside again, making both of them jump. "I'd better get back to my bed," she said. "If I'm caught it'll be the worse for both of us. Grace, you'll soon be free. I'll give Thomas this paper tomorrow and we'll have you out in a blink."

* ✳ *

Thomas had sent his letter to Reverend Woldingham and was now searching through an old trunk in a small room off the props store. It was where he kept his most personal possessions. Nothing valuable that anyone might want to steal, but the things that he held dear. There were his old school books; the hat he had worn for his wedding to poor dear, dead Maud; his twins' cribs.

Thomas was worried and upset. He had felt uneasy ever since returning from the asylum in Balham. He should never have left Rose there. It had been a mad idea. But once Rose had decided something, dissuading her was like trying to take a bone off a terrier.

But he hated leaving Rose, particularly when she was so angry with him. He couldn't bear to think of the way she had stood so stiffly when he had gone to hug her goodbye, and how small and wan she had looked as he'd turned to wave before the door banged behind him. It had seemed so final, as if he might never see her again. He so wished he had told her about what happened when she was a baby before yesterday.

He reached down further into the trunk and his hand grasped what he was looking for: two halves of an old, worn swaddling sheet. Gently, he pulled them out. The material was fragile, but to his relief it was still intact. The moths had stayed away. He studied one sheet and then the other. They were threadbare but anyone could see the quality: the stitching was so delicate. He held one half-sheet up to the light and gave a tiny gasp of surprise. In the very corner, stitched in white thread so it was almost invisible, was a tiny butterfly. He picked up the other half of the sheet and saw the same butterfly motif. The butterfly was the emblem of the Easingford family.

The babies had each been wrapped in this sheet. The babies! Maybe Ned had been asking after "the babies" for a reason. He thought of the envelope with Oliver Dorset's address on it and the names scrawled on the back. Ned had written *Rose and ?* Had Ned—

He heard a sound behind him. He turned round, and as he glimpsed the face in front of him, the past came rushing back.

"You!" he said in astonishment. "It was you!" He tried to get to his feet, and as he did so, a cricket bat hit him on the side of the head. After that he saw and felt nothing.

25

Rose sat in the drawing room at Ivanhoe House watching the clock. Thomas would soon be here to take her away. She would have liked to have tried to see Grace one more time but it was too risky. She patted her pocket, where she was safely keeping Grace's signed note. She hoped that Mr Cherryble was right and it would be enough to get Grace released quickly.

Rose turned over what she knew in her mind. It was obvious that Ned had really loved Grace, so why would he keep her in the dark about his past? He had to be trying to protect her and Freddie. Maybe he had felt that the less they knew, the safer they would be. But that implied he had a dangerous secret.

Rose mused on. Things seemed to have

changed just before his death. Grace had said that Ned was distracted and worried. Grace knew Ned had been to Yorkshire, and Rose knew from the envelope she'd found that Oliver Woldingham had written to Ned too. Grace also knew that Ned had been in correspondence with someone in America. If only they could find out who that was.

The clock chimed noon. Rose stood up and looked out of the window at the curved drive, watching for the carriage that would bring Thomas to release her. She was still standing there four hours later. Thomas had not come for her as promised. She choked back the tears. He had done the very thing that he promised that he would never do: he had abandoned her.

For a moment she wondered if he was punishing her in some way for how she had behaved yesterday in the carriage. But she knew that Thomas had too much generosity of spirit to ever hold a grudge like that. Her heart lurched. Something had happened to him, something terrible.

Suddenly she realised that Dr Fogg had come to stand next to her.

"You see," he said gloatingly. "I was right. It is quite extraordinary how quickly they forget you once they have left you here like an unwanted parcel."

Rose clenched her fists. She wanted to scream and shout, but then she remembered Grace strapped to the bed upstairs. Screaming and shouting would get her nowhere.

"I'm sure my father will have a good reason for his delay. I know he loves me," she said with all the dignity she could muster.

"How very sweet," said Dr Fogg. "But in my experience love can be so very forgetful." He started to walk away. "Oh, and in case you were thinking of trying, the front and back doors are securely locked, and Mrs Gawkin and I are the only ones with keys."

Rose disguised her surprise and tried to keep her voice as calm as she could. "Who is Mrs Gawkin?" she asked.

"Matron," said Dr Fogg shortly. "It is Hannah Gawkin who makes sure this place runs like clockwork." He strode away.

Rose sank down on the chair and stared at the bars on the window. They suddenly seemed to have grown thicker and more menacing. The names that kept coming up had to be more than coincidence. She knew from the silver cup that Lizzie had an Easingford link. Ned had been called an Easingford, even though he denied it. And she had overheard there was a Sarah Easingford here at Ivanhoe House. Rose knew she had to find and talk to her. And now it seemed she had all the time in the world.

* ✳ *

Lizzie sat on Mr Snetherbridge's hard-backed chair and licked her lips. The letter she had written, saying that since she had heard nothing from Mr Snetherbridge she had decided to take her information elsewhere, had obviously done the trick. The threat had been a risky strategy, not least because from now on she would have to be constantly vigilant, watching out for a knife in the ribs late at night on a lonely street. But so far it seemed to be paying off.

She had been quickly summoned to a meeting in Soho Square. In the first few minutes it became apparent to her that Snetherbridge did not have the box containing the silver cup and ribbon and believed that they were still in her possession. But what he and his lordship did not yet realise was that she had an even greater prize. She could produce the child.

Mr Snetherbridge eyed her with distaste. He was still smarting from the volcanic anger with which Lord Henry had exploded when Josiah confirmed that he had seen a butterfly mark on Freddie Dorset's neck. He'd been furious that Josiah had allowed the child to slip through his fingers and now couldn't locate him even though he had apparently been keeping a close eye on Campion's. Without the child they would have to continue to negotiate with Lizzie Gawkin.

"I think we need to get down to real business, Mrs Gawkin," said Mr Snetherbridge. "His lordship is grateful for the information that you have provided so far."

Lizzie simpered. "I want nothing more, Mr Snetherbridge, than to be a friend to the Easingford family and his lordship."

"And Lord Henry appreciates that, Mrs Gawkin. But he needs further proof that you have his best interests at heart or I'm afraid he will think you are merely bluffing."

"I never bluff," said Lizzie sharply. "You already know that I have the cup and ribbon. What you don't know is how boldly I acted in removing a direct threat to his lordship's reputation."

Mr Snetherbridge waited for more, but Lizzie remained silent.

"If you could just explain yourself a little more clearly, Mrs Gawkin, maybe I could see my way to a small payment for all the trouble you have gone to so far on his lordship's behalf."

He reached into his desk drawer, opened a small box and pushed it towards Lizzie. Lizzie's eyes gleamed with greed. There were at least fifty gold sovereigns in the box, maybe more. This was more like it. She put out her hand, but Mr Snetherbridge moved the box just out of her reach. He leaned forward.

"First things first, Mrs Gawkin."

The gold sovereigns seemed to be winking at Lizzie from the box. They were irresistible. She wanted them.

"I told you that Edward Easingford was dead at our last meeting. What I didn't tell you is that I killed him. I did it for his lordship. I was more familiar with the young man's history than he was himself, and I knew that he was a ghost from the past who could ruin everything for Lord Henry. So I lured him to an alley by the river, hit him over the head and pushed him in. It was quite simple, and done so easily that he could barely have felt a thing."

Mr Snetherbridge disguised his distaste at the pleasure she seemed to take in the murder. But it confirmed everything he already knew about the death of Ned Dorset.

"But of course there is still the child."

"Yes," said Lizzie, "there is the child. But once I have received my full payment – I think a thousand guineas should suffice – I will deliver her to you, and you can do what you want with her. She will be of no further use to me."

"Her!" Mr Snetherbridge gave a yelp of surprise that he then tried to cover with a cough. "The child is a girl?"

Lizzie smiled. "Aurora Scarletti, the Infant Phenomenon, is the daughter of Edward Easingford. I have the evidence to prove it. Why else would I have looked after the brat for all these years?"

"Of course," said Mr Snetherbridge, trying to collect his thoughts. "You have the child, the documents, the cup and the ribbon. But no doubt you are aware that there is one further thing that will conclusively prove the truth of what you are saying."

"What is that?"

"The Easingford butterfly. I suppose she has the mark on her neck?"

For a split second Lizzie stared at him dumbstruck, and then very smoothly before he could notice she leaned forward and said, "But of course."

Her mind was racing. A butterfly birthmark on Aurora's neck? She had never noticed one. Even though she had always had as little physically to do with the child as possible, leaving her to tend and dress herself, she was sure she would have noticed something like that. Maybe she *had* got the wrong child. She just had to hold her nerve and keep bluffing. She looked longingly at the money in the open box, but Mr Snetherbridge stood up and snapped it shut.

"Mrs Gawkin," he said with a thin smile. "His lordship will be most grateful to you, and I will be in touch to arrange where and how we might complete an agreement."

The pimply boy appeared to escort her to the front door. As Lizzie Gawkin trotted off down the street, Lord Henry appeared from his nook where he had been listening.

"That woman is deluded," he said. "Josiah Pinch was quite certain that Ned Dorset only had one child, a son. Who is this other child? If I hadn't touched her cold, stiff body myself, I'd be expecting my sister-in-law, Lily, to suddenly knock at the door too."

Mr Snetherbridge frowned. "Maybe Lizzie Gawkin is deluded but maybe she isn't. It's not impossible that there could be two children. I have heard of this music-hall act, Aurora Scarletti, the so-called Infant Phenomenon. She is older than Grace Dorset's boy. Perhaps your nephew fathered her, and then abandoned her and the mother?"

"A girl is less of a problem, in that she can have no claim against the title. But if she *is* the child of Edward Easingford she must be dealt with as her very existence would be awkward, and she could make a claim against her grandmother Lily's fortune. Remove both the children. If either of them ever came forward I would never make Privy Council and the ancient Easingford name would be blackened forever. I would rather die than let that happen."

"Perhaps Lizzie Gawkin will dispatch

two children for the price of one?" said Mr Snetherbridge quietly.

"Perhaps that bloodthirsty vixen will. She seemed quite pleased with the way she killed Edward. But I'm not complaining. She has done me a favour and finished the job I bungled at his birth."

26

It was twenty-four hours after Thomas had been found unconscious, a bloodstained cricket bat by his fallen body. Aurora and Effie were hiding in some bushes, gazing at the high, forbidding wall that surrounded Ivanhoe House. They had walked around it twice and found no obvious way in. But they were determined to rescue Rose, not only for her sake but also for Thomas's.

"Maybe it's a blessing Thomas can't recall a thing that happened after he had his breakfast yesterday," said Aurora. "If he knew that he had left Rose in the asylum, and that she was trapped there until he was well enough to go there himself and claim her, he'd go insane with worry." She blushed at her unfortunate choice

237

of words. "He keeps asking for her. He's going to realise something's up very soon."

"Maybe if we rescue Rosie, seeing her will make Thomas remember what happened. He only had an old linen sheet in his hand, and that's not the sort of thing somebody tries to kill you for," said Effie.

Aurora sighed. "And just imagine how Rose must be feeling. She must think she's been abandoned. We can't even get her a message."

"Come on," said Effie. "Let's have another look round."

The two girls walked past a small wooden door in the wall on which a faded notice was pinned. "Hang on," said Effie, pointing to it. "What's that say?"

Aurora read it out. *"Maid of all work required. Ring bell at front gates."*

Effie's eyes lit up. "It's worth a try," she said, clutching Aurora's arm excitedly. "I can find Rose and Grace, and get 'em out! I'll steal the keys if I have to."

It was decided. Effie would knock and ask after the job, while Aurora raced back to Campion's. If Effie didn't show up later, Aurora would get the horse and cart and return with it after midnight, ready to pick up brave Effie and the others.

* ✳ *

Rose chewed her fingernails and paced the drawing room. It was long past suppertime. Nobody would come for her tonight, of that she was certain. She was worried sick about Thomas. Something terrible must have happened to him. She came to a rest in front of the barred window, and she saw reflected in the glass a woman she hadn't seen before shuffle into the room behind her. Could it be?

"Sarah?" asked Rose gently. "Are you Sarah Easingford?"

The woman nodded and put an arm out towards Rose, tears falling down her face. Rose guided the woman to the sofa and the two of them sank into it. The woman touched Rose's face. "Who are you, child? Do I know you?"

Rose took the woman's hand, stroking it gently, and thought of the things she knew about the Easingford family.

"I'm Rose. I know who you are. You were Sarah Charlotte Dorset and your sister was called Lily."

The woman smiled gently. There wasn't a hint

of madness in her eyes, only sorrow.

"Nobody has called me Sarah Dorset for years. Not since I was a girl. Not since I married my husband, who had me stuck inside here after the birth of our son, Edgar. But me and Lily, we were the Dorset sisters. Everybody knew the Dorset sisters."

"Tell me more about Lily," said Rose softly. "What happened to her?"

A faraway look came into Sarah's eyes. "I've tried to tell people for years but nobody listens. They just think I'm raving."

"I'll listen. I want to hear what you have to say," whispered Rose.

"Lily didn't want to marry Frederick Easingford. She wanted to marry Oliver Woldingham, our cousin. But he was just a poor parson and Frederick Easingford had a title and an estate. She was given no choice by my father. She didn't love Frederick, although he was a kind enough man." She stopped and her features contorted. "Not like his twin brother, *my* husband." She leaned in to Rose and whispered, "Henry is the very devil."

The woman seemed lost in thought for a moment, before she continued.

"So Lily married Frederick, but she still loved Oliver and he loved her. Oliver was the parson at Easingford Church, my dear, and he had to see her every day. How they both suffered! But then Frederick died shortly after the wedding. He was out riding alone with his brother, Henry, when it happened. I've always wondered if his death might not have been the accident Henry said it was. It gave Oliver and Lily hope they might eventually marry. But Lily was expecting Frederick's child, a child who, if he was a boy, would be the next Lord Easingford."

Sarah sighed. "I was living at Easingford Hall too. My father, Lord Dorset, had died, and I was the ward of my sister's husband, a duty that passed to Henry when Frederick died. It was a difficult time. Henry made it clear he thought the title should be his. During the last six months of her confinement he made Lily's life hell. It was as if he was trying to kill her. But then nature did his job for him. She succumbed to the influenza and died giving birth."

Rose squeezed Sarah's hand. "I'm so sorry. To lose your sister and her son like that must have been a terrible blow."

"But – and this is what no one believes – the

child *didn't* die. Everyone thought he was dead, but Henry didn't do a good enough job of smothering him. The child lived."

Rose looked shocked. "How can you be certain he tried to kill the baby?"

"I saw it all with my own eyes," said Sarah. "I'd long learned that the way to survive at Easingford Hall was to watch without being seen. It made me quite the little spy. I was hiding behind a Chinese screen in his bedroom. I saw him with the pillow. Later I was hidden behind the dining-room curtains when the coffin was on the table. Henry put the baby into the coffin with my poor dead sister. He watched while the coffin was nailed up and then he left, thinking the job had been done, and that's when we heard the cry."

"We?" asked Rose.

"The coffin maker, Joe, and his wife, Abigail. They didn't know I was there either. When Henry left, they pulled off the coffin lid and removed the swaddled baby and the silver cup and ribbon that Henry had placed in the coffin too. They were never seen again. They were good people. They knew that Henry would kill the boy if he discovered he was still alive. They saved Edward, my sister's son."

Rose's mouth was hanging open. She was now absolutely certain that she knew who Ned Dorset had been. He was Lily's son, which meant that Freddie was the rightful heir to Easingford. That placed him in more danger than ever. Rose knew she had to get away from Ivanhoe House and back to Campion's as soon as possible.

"Do you know what happened to Joe and Abigail and the baby?" she asked.

The old woman shook her head. "But Oliver might. He always promised me he would try to find out. Oliver is a man who keeps his promises."

"Sarah, tell me one more thing. How did you come to marry Henry, especially after all you'd seen?"

Bitterness flooded Sarah's features. "I had no choice. I was his ward. It was a forced marriage. He cared less for me than he did for his dog, and he beat me more often. He wanted my fortune and he wanted a son and heir. I gave him both. Two weeks after I gave birth to Edgar he announced that I was to have minimal contact with my own son. He was to be raised away from me in the London house in Silver Square before being sent away to school. The loss was too much to bear and my breaking heart made me reckless. I told him that I knew that his nephew lived. He had me committed here, knowing no one would believe the words of a mad woman shut up in an asylum because her husband, a great lord, said she was insane."

Rose gave her a huge hug. "I believe you, Sarah, and I'm going to try to prove the truth of it."

A maid came into the room as Rose sat thinking. "There's cocoa upstairs," she said.

Rose's head flew up at the familiar voice. "Effie?"

Effie put a finger to her lips. "I'll tell you everything. But first I need to get you and Grace out of here."

27

Oliver Dorset Woldingham stood in the graveyard of Easingford Church, holding two letters that had arrived that morning. His head was reeling.

One was from Chicago. It included some newspaper cuttings, glowing reviews of a young English actor called Ed Ford who had taken the city by storm playing Hamlet. Edward Easingford's face smiled from a cutting. He looked barely older than he had thirteen years ago when Oliver had waved him off on the boat to America. The young man had been grief-stricken then. Oliver was thrilled that he was doing so well in Chicago, although he knew that all the success in the world could never make up for the terrible loss of his child.

He turned to the other letter again. This one was far more troubling. It was from a Thomas Campion, and it contained the terrible news that Ned Dorset was dead. Murdered. Oliver put his face in his hands. He wondered if his actions had played a part in Ned's death. He remembered when the boy had come to him in such pain and distress thirteen years ago, and their meeting just after Christmas when Oliver had told him everything that had happened on that long ago day following Lily Easingford's death.

Ned had been fired up with what he saw as a terrible injustice and was determined to right the wrong, whatever the cost to himself. Now it seemed he had paid a high price for trying to uncover the truth. Thomas Campion was asking urgently for information, and saying that Ned's wife and child were in danger too. Oliver shivered. Henry Easingford had already destroyed the two Dorset sisters and now it seemed he'd thrown his malevolent web over the next generation as well.

Oliver knew he must go to London at once. He walked over to the corner of the churchyard and the low grassy mound covered in wild daffodils, known as Lent lilies. The first buds of spring were just visible on the oriental lilies that he had planted by the wall by the knoll. He hoped that the cruel frost wouldn't nip them, and they would bloom longer than Lily and Ned had done.

Oliver knelt on the grassy mound, and thought about the night thirty-two years ago he'd spent digging alone in the dark churchyard, wild with grief. How he'd uncovered the coffin of Lily, his beloved, whose funeral service he had presided over that afternoon. The Easingford family had stolen her from him, but he was determined that they would not own her in death. He had simply been going to rebury the coffin in the sunny side of the churchyard in the unmarked grave he had dug for her and which he planned to smother with flowers. But the desire to look upon the face of the woman he loved one last time had been too strong. He had opened the coffin.

Subsequent snatched meetings on the moor with Sarah Dorset had told him all he needed to know about what he'd found inside. Sarah had then been shut away in an asylum for telling the truth. Now he had to tell the world what had really happened. He bent and kissed the grassy mound.

"Oh, Lily, Lily. No more secrets, my love." He sniffed the air. For a moment he thought that it was filled with the sweet scent of summer lilies, but he knew that he must have imagined it.

* ✖ *

Ivanhoe House's patients had all been sent to bed. Effie was scrubbing the cocoa pot and cups and saucers in the scullery. The door to the kitchen was open. Hannah Gawkin and the cook, Ruby Breton, were sitting at the kitchen table, gossiping.

"Ever hear word of your sister, Han?" asked Ruby.

Effie put down the pot as quietly as she could and crept closer to the door to listen.

"Who? Lizzie, Bess, Bet? Don't even know which name she calls herself these days. Haven't laid eyes on her since she scarpered with our little Dawnie," said Hannah with a bitter laugh. "Such a lovely little thing, and right precocious she was, always dancing and singing out on them black-and-white tiles in the hall as if it was her own personal stage. She even made Dr Fogg smile. I reckon Lizzie saw a way to turn a penny from Dawnie in the music halls, and went back to that way of life. I loved that little kid, Ruby. Did everything for her, looked after her like the child I never had. It broke my heart when Lizzie took off with her like that. It was like losing a daughter. If my sister turned up now, I'd call the rozzers. Reckon she wouldn't like that one bit."

"Even though she's your own flesh and blood?" said Ruby.

"I know it sounds harsh. Lizzie was my little sister but she grew up bad, through and through," said Hannah. "Four husbands and all of 'em dead within the year. Ain't natural, if you ask me."

"And what about that scandal when she turned up here all those years ago," said Ruby, who was enjoying these confidences.

"Yes, well, she was never one to stay and face the music. She'd been working as a dresser at that hall down Bermondsey way where that tenor got murdered. Victorious, I think it was called. She came here with a long sob story about losing her job and how it wasn't her fault. But I think she'd been up to her old tricks. Petty thieving, a bit of blackmail. I took her in, told her it could only be for a few days. Thought she could help out; we were short-handed as usual."

"We always are," said Ruby. "People thinks they'll be tainted by working in the mad house."

"Course, Lizzie was no help at all. She was always hanging round Sarah Easingford. I got quite shirty with her, particularly when I caught her with a silver cup. Red-handed, she were. I reckon the cup was why she was here – she'd prigged it and wanted somewhere safe to lie low. I was going to send her on her way. Was pleased when she said she was going away."

"But she came back?"

Hannah nodded. "She disappeared for a couple of days and turned up back here with a little baby. Dawnie. One peep and I was lost. She said the child belonged to a friend who'd died. I doubted it was true, but the babe was such a sweet thing. So they both stayed. Then five years later she skips off with the little 'un without a word and broke my heart."

Hannah wiped a tear from her eye and then yelled towards the scullery.

"You finished them pots, Edie?"

"Just done," called Effie.

"That girl could be a bit of a find, even if she

did come without a reference. A good little worker. Nifty with her fingers too." Hannah yawned. "Right, bed for me."

"Me an' all," said Ruby. The two women got laboriously to their feet and shuffled off towards the stairs.

Effie bit her lip. She was going to have to be *very* nifty with her fingers tonight, and no mistake.

* ❋ *

Effie tiptoed into Hannah Gawkin's room. Hannah was fast asleep on her back, the keys hanging from the bedpost above her head. Effie grimaced. They would make a noise as soon as she touched them unless she manoeuvred them with real delicacy. She took a step forward. Hannah's breathing remained steady. Trying to stop her hand shaking, Effie very gently started to lift the keys up over the bedpost. Hannah stirred, and Effie froze until Hannah's breathing steadied again. Carefully Effie raised the keys over the bedpost. If she was caught now, she would end up in Holloway. With her spare hand she pulled a piece of linen from her apron pocket and with the lightest of touches wrapped the keys in it in a single movement. There was just the tiniest clink.

She hurried up the stairs to the third floor where Rose had told her Grace was incarcerated. But when she reached the top of the stairs and peered around the corner she saw a nurse sitting on a chair right outside Grace's room.

There was nothing she could do but carry on with the rest of the plan. Effie crept back down the stairs and unlocked the door that led from the public rooms to the kitchen. The grandfather clock in the hall chimed one o'clock as she did so, and a few seconds later Rose appeared at the bottom of the stairs.

"Where's Grace?" she whispered.

"There's a nurse sitting outside her room."

"We can't leave her here!" said Rose desperately.

"Be sensible, Rosie, we have to," said Effie. "If we can get you out with that bit of paper, Mr Cherryble will help her."

Rose opened her mouth to protest but Effie said very firmly, "Do you want to get out of here or not? This is your only chance."

Reluctantly, Rose followed Effie through the door that led to the kitchens and Effie locked it behind them. They hurried through the kitchen to the back door. Once again Effie selected exactly the right key from the bunch (she had been paying careful attention when Hannah Gawkin made her rounds of the house) and it opened soundlessly.

The children tiptoed across the grass, its frosted blades shimmering in the moonlight. They headed to the small back door set in the high wall that surrounded the house. Effie looked at the lock and considered the keys. She tried a long one that was rustier then the others. It slipped into the lock as if it belonged there, but when she tried to turn it, it refused to budge. Fingers trembling, she tried another. No good. A light went on in a window at the back of the house. If anyone looked out of the window now, there was a high chance they would be spotted. Effie went back to the first key. Once again it fitted the lock perfectly. This time Effie pulled the door hard towards her as she attempted to turn the key. The lock turned with a rusty creak. Effie pulled the door open and they moved quickly through it. On the other side Effie pulled the door shut and relocked it. They set off swiftly down the lane where Aurora was waiting with a cart and horse.

Rose threw herself into the cart. "Gee up! I need to see Thomas!"

28

Thomas Campion was sitting at his desk. His head was heavily bandaged but he was feeling much better. If only he could recall more clearly what had happened to him. It worried him that somebody at the theatre had attacked him.

The fog outside was thick tonight, as dense and sticky as porridge. He could see little outside his window, and just occasionally he caught the glimmer of a lantern crossing the yard. At least the fog in his mind was beginning to clear since Rose had returned in the dead of night. She had been sitting by his bed when he awoke. He'd been horrified to learn his bang to the head had left her a helpless prisoner. He had begged Rose's forgiveness, but she had merely hugged him so hard that it hurt quite a lot, and said, "Oh, Thomas, I knew there'd be an explanation for why you hadn't returned, and that you would come back for me when you could because I know you love me like a father."

Thomas and the others had been gripped by Rose's account of her conversation with Sarah Dorset.

"So I think there can be no doubt," said Rose. "Ned Dorset was Lily and Lord Frederick's son, Edward Easingford."

"Which means," said Thomas, "that Freddie is actually the rightful Lord Easingford."

"It's just like a stage melodrama," said Rose. "Even better than the ones you used to write, Thomas."

"Maybe," said Thomas. "But at least in my stories the blood isn't real and nobody actually gets murdered. We're going to have to go to the police."

Rose looked at him astounded. She didn't have much faith in the rozzers, and they'd probably be laughed out of the station. Who would believe their word against that of a great lord, a man about to be made a privy councillor to boot? They needed more evidence. They needed to speak to Oliver Dorset Woldingham.

"There's more," said Rose, and she nudged Effie, who told them what she had heard about Lizzie Gawkin.

Thomas had frowned at the mention of the woman's name. Damn his aching head, he just couldn't remember what it was that made him feel so anxious about her.

Just then, Lottie appeared at the door. She and Gus, the stage manager, had been doing sterling work keeping Campion's going over the last two days and ensuring that the show did indeed go on. "All right, you lot, I need some 'elp downstairs and I bet Thomas needs a rest from your gabbing."

They'd all trooped after her to get ready for the first show, leaving Thomas sitting down at his desk to go over the takings. Houses had been superb the last two nights. Lottie had said that audiences were going mad for the cancan with the small blonde girl called Dora at the end of the line. When word got round that the girls' bicycle act, in which Aurora would appear dressed as a boy for the first time, was back at the top of the bill tonight, both performances were likely to be sell-outs.

Thomas wondered whether Campion's

fortunes might be on the turn. He hoped so. He was expecting Mr Cherryble imminently to discuss the finances and also to mull over what was to be done with Freddie. He could hardly stay hidden as a girl forever. Thomas wondered whether he should send him to his brother in the country for a while. He also wanted to talk to Mr Cherryble about Aurora. He wanted Lizzie out of Campion's as soon as possible but he didn't want her to take Aurora with her. If he had to pay to ensure Lizzie's departure and to keep Aurora as part of the Campion's family, so be it.

But he wanted to be careful. The woman was vindictive, possibly dangerous. He needed her to leave Campion's feeling she had got the upper hand. He felt quite certain she might put a match to Campion's if she felt thwarted.

There was a knock at the door. Thomas said, "Come in, Cherryble." But it was not the lawyer. A man of about fifty with a kind face and cornflower-blue eyes stepped into the room. He was wearing a dog collar. He removed his hat and held out his hand.

"Mr O'Leary said to come up. I'm Oliver Woldingham. I have come, Mr Campion, in response to your letter. I cannot believe that dear

Ned Dorset is dead. I must tell you all I know to avoid further tragedy."

Thomas offered Oliver a seat, and by the time Mr Cherryble joined them, the men were already in deep conversation.

* ✳ *

Josiah Pinch sat at the back of the gallery watching as the cancan came to an end. Around him people were up on their feet, their faces glowing, but Josiah stayed firmly seated, his bowler tilted over his face, just in case those prying children saw him. He still felt certain that Freddie was hidden away at Campion's. He had kept watch, but there had been no sign of the boy; the only child he had seen was a little blonde girl he had glimpsed running around the yard playing with the cat.

Josiah was wondering whether he should follow Lizzie Gawkin's example and get into the blackmail business. If he could only find the boy, maybe he could put the screws on Lord Henry. After all, Josiah knew rather more about his lordship's affairs than he would ever want made public.

The band struck up again. The crowd leaned forward. The tune was "Daisy Bell". The crowd gave a cheer as Rose came on stage riding the bicycle. Josiah grimaced at the sight of it. He still had the bruises where Effie had cycled into him. There was a roar from the crowd as a young boy stepped on stage. Josiah suddenly stood up to get a closer look. It was the same boy he'd seen going into Campion's on the day of the Shoreditch debacle. Only it wasn't a boy, of course. It was that Aurora girl pretending to be a boy! What an idiot he was. What a fool those kids had taken him for, parading Freddie in front of his very nose as little Dora. He stood up and forced his way along the row to the exit. He knew that Freddie Dorset was here. All he had to do now was snatch him.

* ✳ *

Aurora came off stage laughing. The act had gone really well. She loved doing it with Rose. Then they came face to face with Lizzie and her heart sank. She had enjoyed being so free of Lizzie recently, but she knew it couldn't last.

To Aurora's surprise, Lizzie smiled at both the girls and said, "That's a wonderful act you two have worked up. What clever little things you are."

Aurora and Rose were astonished and then

suspicious; it was not like Lizzie to lavish praise. The woman continued, "You look very daring in that get-up, Aurora. And, Rose, you look lovely, my dear. But you ought to wear your hair up." She moved to lift up Rose's hair to reveal her neck but Rose squirmed away.

"Thanks, Lizzie," said Rose, trying not to shudder at the touch of the woman's clammy fingers, "but I need to tighten the screw on this pedal before it drops off." She disappeared with the bicycle.

Lizzie stared after her. "I'm off for a gin," she said, and walked off, leaving Aurora puzzling at her strange behaviour.

Another big bunch of flowers had arrived at the stage door for Tess, so Aurora picked it up and took it down to the ballet girls' dressing room. Tess, Lottie and the others were brewing a huge pot of tea.

"Do you want some, Aurora?" asked Lottie. Aurora shook her head. She was about to leave when she spotted something under a jumble of clothes.

"Oh," she said. "There's my shawl. I wondered where it had gone."

"Is it yours?" asked Lottie. "I borrowed it to

wear to poor Ned's funeral. It was in the trunk with the *Aladdin* props."

Aurora stared at her. She remembered Effie had mentioned a shawl.

"You all right, Aurora? You look as if you've seen a ghost!"

"Lottie," said Aurora urgently, "when you took the shawl, did you take anything else from the trunk?"

Lottie shrugged. "Only an old box. We needed something to keep make-up in but it was locked. It's over there, under Belle's mum's bit of embroidery."

Aurora lifted the embroidered linen and there was the lacquered box.

"Sorry, Lottie," she said, "but I need this."

Aurora ran into the dressing room next door. She got a hatpin and fiddled around with it; after a few seconds she heard a click and the box opened. She pulled out the contents, put the cup and ribbon to one side and began to sift through the papers. A newspaper cutting from *The Times* caught her eye, or at least the photograph did. It was of the young man who had picked up Lizzie's glove outside the post office on the day they had arrived at Campion's. The newspaper said the man was a young English actor called Ed Ford who was taking America by storm. Scrawled in Lizzie's handwriting at the bottom were the words Edward Easingford. The young man at the post office! The day they had arrived at Campion's! The day Ned Dorset died! She gasped, remembering the fleck of blood on Lizzie's glove. Aurora ran next door to Lottie's dressing room.

"Lottie," she said, holding her hand over the story so all that Lottie could see was the photograph. "Lottie, do you know who this is?"

Lottie glanced at the picture. "Course I do," she said. "Know 'im anywhere. That's poor dead Ned Dorset."

Aurora raced back to her dressing room, where she picked up the lacquered box and its contents to take it to show Rose, Thomas and the others. She flung open the door again and came face to face with an unsmiling Lizzie.

29

"Well, well, well," said Lizzie. "It seems that my box isn't lost after all. How very, very convenient for me, and how extremely inconvenient for you." She produced a long stiletto. "Scream and this knife will find your heart."

Aurora was terrified by the wild look in Lizzie's eye. "Please don't hurt me, Auntie," she whispered.

"Auntie! Don't make me laugh. You're no relative of mine." Lizzie poked the knife at Aurora's ribs and gave a cruel laugh. "I've no idea who you are, but you're certainly not who I thought you might be. You're just some little nobody I stole out of a pram in the West End. I have no further need for you. My interests now lie elsewhere."

"Please," whispered Aurora. "Please let me go."

Lizzie sneered. "Don't take me for a fool. You're not going anywhere."

* ✳ *

Upstairs, Oliver Woldingham was still telling his story.

"Eventually I managed to trace the coffin maker and his wife. It took many years and many false leads. They made sure that they disappeared into the crowd to keep the baby safe. They changed their name to Ford, a common enough name, and called the boy Ed.

"Abigail died within a couple of years of arriving in London. But Joe looked after the boy and loved him like a son. He got a job making scenery in a hall in Lambeth, and that's how his son became an actor. By the time I found Joe, Ed was away working in theatres north of the border and had married a Scottish girl called Louisa. He and his wife knew nothing of his history, and Joe didn't want them to know anything. He told me that he had given his son the silver cup and ribbon as a wedding present, saying they had been given to him for good service, and that the cup was worth very little, but that Edward should value it as it linked him to his Yorkshire heritage.

"Joe was a sick man by the time I found him, and troubled by what he and Abigail had done. He wanted to make a confession to me. I wrote down the full history of all that had passed and I have the signed confession here. Joe died quite suddenly and I vowed I would do everything in my power to help Lily's son. But Edward was in London and had learned of Joe's death by the time I met him. Then something terrible happened to him, something from which I feared he would never recover..."

* ✳ *

Josiah Pinch cast a furtive look around to check that nobody was nearby, although the fog was so thick it was hard to see beyond the length of your arm. A small pool of honeyed light spilled out from the half-open stage door. He could see O'Leary's feet stretched out on a chair situated just inside the door. Josiah produced a bunch of flowers from behind his back. O'Leary was half snoozing. He had obviously been on the drink. He looked up.

"I'll take those," he said, showing no sign he recognised Josiah from his previous visit.

"Who they for?"

"The tall dark one, Lottie."

"Lovely girl, Lottie. On stage now."

"I'd love to see how the show looks from the side of the stage," said Josiah.

O'Leary shook his head. "Not allowed, I'm afraid."

Josiah produced a small bottle of brandy. "Just a tiny peek?"

O'Leary looked at the brandy. It was good-quality stuff. He reached out and his fingers closed around the neck of the bottle. "Just a quick look then," he said with a wink.

Josiah hurried through into the light. He glanced around, headed down the corridor and pushed open a door. It was the ballet girls' dressing room. Curled up sleepily on a chair was the little blonde child they were calling Dora.

Josiah leaned down towards the child. "Freddie," he said. "It *is* Freddie, isn't it?"

The child sat up. "How do you know my name?" He felt he had seen this man before somewhere but he was too tired to remember where.

"Your mama told me," said Josiah.

The child's eyes opened wide. "You know my mama?"

Josiah nodded. "She's a good friend of mine. Would you like to see her?"

Freddie beamed.

"I'll take you to her," said Josiah. He could hear the music reaching a crescendo. The ballet girls would be back soon; he had to be quick. He held out his hand and Freddie took his finger. They hurried down the corridor. It was unusually quiet. They stopped just before the door.

"Freddie," whispered Josiah. "You do want to see your mama, don't you?"

Freddie nodded.

"Then wait here for a minute and let me go first, then come out into the yard. If O'Leary tries to stop you just tell him you want to give the cat a stroke and you'll be right back. Then I'll take you straight to see your mother."

Freddie knew he was not allowed out in the yard on his own; Rose and the others had explained that to him. But he so wanted to see his mum. He missed her so, and he was tired of being dressed up as a silly girl called Dora. He nodded at the man with the horrid moustache.

Josiah Pinch walked to the door and smiled

pleasantly at O'Leary, who was well into the brandy.

"Thank you, sir. A wonderful show." He disappeared into the fog.

A few seconds later, Freddie trundled past. O'Leary had no idea that Dora was Freddie but he did know the child was not to be allowed outside on her own. He put out a leg to stop Freddie.

"Where are you going, little 'un? You know you're not allowed out there."

"I just want to see Ophelia," said Freddie. "I can hear her mewing for me."

O'Leary smiled. He knew how fond Dora was of that cat. Couldn't stand it himself, mind. "Just for a moment then. Check kitty is all right, then come straight back in. It's too murky a night to be out long."

O'Leary watched as Freddie disappeared into the fog, then he took another swig of brandy and he fell into a doze.

* ✳ *

"Rose!" Lottie's face was scared. "It's Freddie. He's gone. We can't find him anywhere."

"Gone! When?"

"Must have been while we were on stage. He

was in the dressing room. We thought he'd be all right. He was asleep."

"Where have you looked?"

"Everywhere. I thought I heard a sound in the next-door dressing room but he wasn't there. We've looked everywhere backstage."

"I'll get the others," said Rose. "We'll search again. Maybe he crawled under the stage. Or got into the auditorium."

Within seconds everyone except Molly, who was on stage doing her act, was engaged in the search.

"Effie, go upstairs and tell Thomas that Freddie is missing." Rose frowned. "I haven't seen Aurora either. Maybe he's with her."

Rose rushed to the stage door and woke the snoozing O'Leary. "Have you seen little Dora?"

"Eh? Oh, yes," said O'Leary. "She went to see that dratted puss. Ain't she come back yet?"

Rose had to stop herself shaking O'Leary. Instead she asked, "Was anyone else here?"

O'Leary began to explain about the man with the moustache, but Rose didn't wait to hear him finish. "Tell Lottie, O'Leary! I'm going after them." And she was off across the yard like a streak of lightning.

* ✴ *

Effie could hear voices coming from Thomas's office as she raced up the stairs.

"So," Oliver was saying to Thomas and Mr Cherryble, "I told Ned Dorset everything I knew. He was determined to find the lost child and then confront Lord Easingford."

Effie burst into the room just as Thomas, his face as pale as the bandage around his head, jumped to his feet. "The babies!" he said. "It was Lizzie Gawkin who—"

"Freddie's gone missing!" Effie cried.

Immediately the three men started for the stairs. Downstairs, it was mayhem as everyone turned the place upside down. Lottie was waving at Molly to prolong her act. O'Leary was looking bemused.

"If you're looking for Rose, there's no point," he said, trying to be helpful. "She said she's gone after Dora and the man with the moustache."

"Josiah Pinch!" said Effie and Thomas together.

"Did Aurora go with her?" asked Effie.

O'Leary shook his head. Thomas nodded to Lottie. "You're in charge again, Lottie. We're going after Rose and Freddie. They're in terrible danger." He shivered. "My guess is that Josiah will be heading for his lordship's house in Silver Square. We must find them before they get there."

30

Rose ran through the cobbled streets. Few people were about. The fog was so thick it clutched at your throat as if it was trying to suffocate you. She stopped for a moment and thought she heard a child's cry coming from the river. But she could also hear the distinctive *click clack click* of footsteps hurrying in the other direction. She hesitated for a second. Which way to go? Her heart made her want to run towards the river, but her head said to follow the sound of the footsteps. Stealthily she continued onwards. The footsteps headed over the bridge and then turned west. Rose peered into the fog. What if she was following the wrong person? She'd have lost Josiah and Freddie completely. She stopped and listened, and then she heard an unmistakable sob: "Mummy. I want my mummy."

She knew she was on the right track. She followed the footsteps again, grateful there was so little traffic about to disguise the sound. She was suddenly certain that Josiah was taking Freddie to Silver Square. Caught up in following Josiah Pinch, she didn't notice that somebody was following her.

* ✷ *

Aurora had just managed to free her bound hands but she was still locked in the trunk. Her feet were tied and she couldn't reach them, but she pulled away the gag, and started to shout and bang as loudly as she could on the side of the trunk. She yelled and yelled, but the ballet girls were on stage and nobody heard.

Lottie was watching the act. There was a tiny lull in the music and she thought she heard somebody shout "help". It was very faint. She walked briskly down the corridor and it became louder. It was coming from Lizzie and Aurora's dressing room.

"Aurora?"

"In the trunk," came the muffled reply.

Lottie tried the lid. It was locked. Lottie pulled

out a hairpin and within seconds she had it open. She helped Aurora climb out.

"Rose? Where's Rose?" Aurora asked urgently.

"Missing," said Lottie. "Everyone thinks Freddie has been kidnapped by someone called Josiah Pinch, and Rose has given chase."

"I've got to go after them," said Aurora. "I'm certain that Lizzie is going to try and kidnap Rose, maybe even kill her."

* ✳ *

Josiah stopped outside the large white Georgian house with wide steps leading up to an imposing portico. The fog was patchier here than it was on the south side of the river and there were a few more people about. Freddie was whimpering quietly. He no longer believed that this horrid man who had slung him roughly across his shoulder as soon as he went out into the yard was taking him to see his mother. He wanted to go back to the warmth and brightness of Campion's and see Rose and the others.

Josiah kept his arm around the boy's neck while he scribbled a note, informing Lord Easingford that he was here with the boy. He'd show him the child as proof, and offer to dispose of him once and for all for a good price. It would only take a minute or two, and then he would disappear with the cash.

There were a couple of youths lolling by the railings of a house further down the street. He whistled, and they came running. He handed them the folded note and a coin. "Bring me a reply."

The youths ran up the steps and rang the bell. The door opened. A butler took the note and closed the door. Shortly afterwards, he returned with a note and gave it to the boys. They passed it to Josiah who ordered them to scarper.

Hidden behind a tree in the square, Rose watched as Josiah looked at the note and started dragging Freddie around the side of the square. Rose guessed that he was going to the back of the house. She followed. If she just bided her time, maybe she would be able to grab Freddie and make a run for it.

She saw Josiah disappear into a wide alleyway that ran down the back of the row of houses from one end to the other. The houses all had long walled gardens, each with a small gate set in a brick arch in the wall that backed on to the alley. Josiah loitered outside one, whistling

"Pop Goes the Weasel" under his breath. Noise spilled from another house several doors along. Somebody was having a party.

The fog was much thicker in the alleyway, and while Josiah had his back to her Rose risked creeping along it, hoping the noise from the open window at the other house would mask any sound she made. She slipped into the small brick arch of a nearby gate and leaned back against the door, hardly daring to breathe. Rose guessed that Josiah was waiting for someone from the house, presumably Lord Easingford himself, to appear through the door in the wall of the garden.

She leaned back as far as she could so she was squashed like a starfish. Josiah was looking right towards the spot where she was hidden. If it weren't for the swirling fog, Rose was certain that he would have spotted her in the shadows. If he came much closer he almost certainly would. He took a step forward towards her. Then another. Rose's heart began to beat so loudly that she feared Josiah would be able to hear it. He took another step forward. At the next step it would be all over. He moved, and at the same time a look of utter astonishment passed across his face, and then he toppled forward, stone dead. Lizzie stood in the spot where he had been standing, a long thin knife in her hand. The blade was dipped crimson and she held a wriggling Freddie by the scruff of his neck.

"I know you're there, Rose," she said. "Come out or I'll kill the child."

Rose stepped slowly forward from her hiding place, her eyes wide with horror and shock, and at that moment the gate opened and his lordship appeared. He took in the body of Josiah with the bloody wound in his back, Lizzie with the knife at Freddie's throat, and Rose, quiet and watchful.

"Ah, Mrs Gawkin," he said pleasantly, glancing at Josiah's body. "I see that you are quite as ruthless as I have always imagined you would be, so it's lucky that I brought protection." Lord Henry produced a small pistol from his pocket. Lizzie didn't bat an eyelid. He signalled to Rose to move closer to Lizzie so they were standing side by side. Rose put a soothing hand on Freddie's shoulder.

"M'lud, I am only looking after your best interests. My price is a very reasonable one. Give me what I ask, and you can have the girl."

Rose frowned. What could Lizzie possibly mean? Freddie's blonde wig had long since slipped from his head. There was no doubt that he was a boy.

Lord Henry smiled. "Dear Mrs Gawkin, I'm so very delighted that you have delivered both the children in whom I have an interest."

Lizzie frowned as if she had no idea what he meant by both children, but his lordship continued, "Now, hand over the cup and ribbon."

"I want my money first," said Lizzie.

"I'm sure you do," said Lord Henry, "but as I have the gun I think you would be wise to do as I ask." Lizzie raised her knife threateningly. "Go ahead, Mrs Gawkin. Finish them both off; you would be doing me a favour as you did when you killed Edward Easingford."

Lizzie glowered. Her threats counted for nothing in this situation. She didn't understand what interest Lord Henry had in this Freddie, the son of a common music-hall actor. But she would humour him and still hope to come out of the encounter alive and with something in her pocket. She reached into her cloak for the cup and ribbon and as she did so Freddie bit her hard on the arm and broke away. Rose launched herself forward and hit Lizzie full in the stomach. Lizzie doubled over in pain and sank to the ground, trying in vain to catch her breath.

Freddie took off, running down the alleyway and disappearing into the fog. Lord Easingford hesitated for a second, pointed the gun at Rose but then seemed to think better of it and took off after Freddie. It was the boy he wanted.

Rose scooped up the fallen cup and ribbon and ran after Lord Easingford. Lizzie struggled to her feet and followed them all.

31

"Freddie!" shouted Rose. Her heart was pounding. "It's me, Rose!"

There was no answer. She rounded the corner into the square and saw Freddie heading into a small side street. Lord Henry was hard behind and catching him up. The fog suddenly cleared, leaving yellowish will-o'-the-wisp trails. It was a dead end. His lordship stood at the end of the street against a brick wall with Freddie struggling in his arms.

"Stay where you are," he growled at Rose. She fixed him with her slate-dark eyes just as she would a rowdy audience at Campion's. Often a look alone could quieten and calm them.

"Rose!" yelled Freddie, and she could hear the fear in his voice.

"Keep calm, Freddie. I'm here," she said soothingly. She kept her eyes fixed on the man and took a small steady step forward. A mistake.

"I told you not to move," snarled his lordship, and he held the pistol to Freddie's head, the metal glinting against the boy's white skin.

"Please," said Rose. "Give me Freddie. He's done nothing to hurt you. Let him go. He's just a child."

Lord Henry gave a bitter laugh. "But he's not just a child, is he? Oh no. He's the past come back to haunt me and take away my future, and my son's future. He is the child who should never have been born and whose very existence mocks me and destroys everything I have plotted and planned for."

"I hope all the plotting and planning has made you happy," said Rose quietly. She knew it was risky but she hoped her directness might disarm him, catch him off guard. If she could keep him talking perhaps she would have a chance of grabbing Freddie from him.

Lord Henry stared at her, startled by her response. "You cannot possibly understand what it feels like to be the second son of a great titled family. To know that one day your older brother will inherit everything: title, house, land, fortune. Everything. And you will have nothing. That he is the heir and that you are the spare. My brother and I were twins. He was born just seven minutes before me. But what a difference those seven minutes meant to our fates. He was the elder son, the chosen one. I was nothing. Growing up I was certain there had been a mix-up at our births. That I was the true heir and he the usurper. I was certain that eventually someone would realise. I knew that I deserved Easingford and the title more than he did. I loved Easingford so much more than him. But nobody seemed to notice; Frederick remained the chosen one. He inherited the title. I was just a nobody."

"Like me," said Rose softly.

"Then fate, which made me the younger son, played into my hands. My brother died. Now everything I had so long desired was within my grasp. But then his widow announced that she was with child. It was a crushing blow but there was still hope. If the child was a girl, she would merely inherit some of her mother's wealth, but I would still get the title, house and land. But if the child was a boy, once again I would lose out to my brother."

"And you weren't prepared to let that happen," whispered Rose.

Lord Henry shook his head. He seemed much calmer now, as if talking had soothed him.

"At the time the baby was due, an influenza epidemic was raging across the county. Luck was on my side again. Lily, my brother's widow, caught the disease. It seemed likely that she would die before the baby could be born. But she survived just long enough to have a son: Edward. A mewling little thing. It was not hard to smother my nephew and bury him with his mother in Easingford churchyard.

"But fate was laughing at me yet again. It seems that the child survived, rescued from the coffin by the coffin maker and his wife. Lily's sister, Sarah, my ward, was witness to the miraculous escape. She chose to share this information with me after I'd married her for her money and she'd produced Edgar, our son. I decided the best place for her was a mental asylum where no one would believe a word she said. I had no reason to believe what she was saying myself. After all, I'd seen the child being nailed up in the coffin with his mother with my own eyes.

For many years all seemed well. But then my son, Edgar, ran away from school. Of course I put investigators on to the matter immediately. They scoured the country and fortunately they were clever enough to check the ships' passenger lists at all major ports. On one ship travelling to America they found the name Ed Ford. I was sure it was him. To this day I don't know how he got the money for the passage. From the moment he stepped off the boat in New York I have had him watched. I knew that I would yet lure him back and make him face up to his responsibilities as my heir and custodian of an ancient title and great estate.

"Then that blackmailing Lizzie Gawkin appeared and the ghosts began to rise. My dead brother's son came back to haunt me. Conveniently he was murdered by Lizzie Gawkin; she told me so herself with some pride. But it turned out that he had a son of his own. This child. I can see the butterfly mark on his neck that proves he is a true Easingford."

Lord Henry suddenly tensed as footsteps approached. "I have fought for what was rightfully mine and I'm not going to let it go. This child must die. My brother snatched the prize from me and I'm not going to have it snatched again by his grandson."

"But he's not your brother's grandson, he's *your* grandson," came a quiet voice out of the fog. "Freddie isn't Edward's son, he's Edgar's."

Thomas, Mr Cherryble and the man who had spoken, Oliver Woldingham, stepped into view. Two policemen followed, with a struggling, snarling Lizzie Gawkin in their grasp.

Lord Henry started when he saw the parson. "You lie," he scowled. "Edgar is in America. The investigators showed me a photograph of him on the gangplank in New York disembarking from the ship. It was blurred but it was definitely him."

"I'm afraid you are mistaken," replied Oliver. "The boy who went to America almost thirteen years ago was your nephew, Edward, the boy you thought you'd put safely in his grave. He is almost three years older than your own son, Edgar, but the resemblance is considerable. I gave him the money to start his new life after he had suffered a terrible tragedy in London. His wife had died shortly after giving birth and his newborn daughter was stolen away by the woman he had entrusted to look after her temporarily and to whom he had given the only things he had to offer her, a silver cup and a ribbon."

"So where did my son go?" asked Lord Henry, frowning.

"He came to me," said Oliver, "after he ran away from school. Someone at his school had found out that his mother, Sarah, was in a mental asylum. You had lied to him and told him that she had died at his birth, and he wanted to know the truth. I confirmed that she did indeed live. We both tried to visit her at Ivanhoe House but were thwarted. After that he was quite determined never to return to school or to Easingford Hall. He wanted nothing more to do with you or his old life. I respected that. I had seen how the poor boy had grown up motherless and unloved, and yet had remained true of heart and spirit. I told him nothing of his cousin. I felt it was safer for both boys to know as little as possible. After all, you had already proved yourself prepared to murder an innocent babe. What might you do to anyone who knew of this crime? Even if it was your own son?

"I gave Edgar what small amount of money I could, he chose a new name from the graveyard and I sent him out into the world to make his way as an actor. We kept in touch. Then he contacted me. He had seen a review of a performance in Chicago by Ed Ford and thought that the resemblance and the name were too much of a coincidence. He was curious. Years had passed; both boys had grown into mature young men. So I told him the truth and put him in correspondence with his cousin in America. Your son was a good man, a very good man and he was determined to try and find Edward's stolen child if she was still alive. He wrote to me shortly after Christmas saying he was certain that he was close to identifying the child and would be in touch soon. I never heard from him again, and only discovered a few days ago that he had been murdered."

"The name he was using?" said Lord Henry brokenly, already sure of the answer.

"Ned. Ned Dorset," said Oliver.

Henry Easingford's face slackened and he let Freddie go. The boy ran to Rose, who scooped him into her arms and cradled him.

"Ned Dorset? I never killed no Ned Dorset,"

said Lizzie wildly. "Never met him in me life."

"Yes, you did," said Aurora, who had been standing quietly at the back of the group for a while. "We met him by unfortunate chance outside the post office on the morning we arrived at Campion's. Because of his resemblance to his cousin, Edward, you mistook him for the bereaved man who'd asked you to look after his baby. Quickly, you decided to murder him before he identified you as the woman who had stolen his child just when all your plans to blackmail Lord Easingford were coming to fruition. Only of course, he wasn't the man you took him for: he was Edgar Easingford."

"My son," said his lordship, and grief seemed suddenly to envelop him like a shroud.

"Lies!" shouted Lizzie. "Damnable lies!"

"No, they're not," said Thomas, putting his arm around Aurora's thin shoulders. "It was you I saw through the window of my study when you came back for the babies you left on the steps of Campion's all those years ago. I didn't recognise you at first when you arrived at Campion's with Aurora. But I did remember later, and that's why you attacked me and tried to kill me. I'm certain that you tried to take both babies because you didn't know which of the two was Edward Easingford's daughter."

Lizzie gave a nasty little laugh. "You're right. I had no idea which one was a lord's daughter and which one was a nasty little nobody stolen out of a pram in the West End."

"So," whispered Rose, coming to stand next to Aurora, "which one of us is Edward Easingford's lost baby?"

Lizzie brayed like a sick donkey. "Well, it's not that stupid Aurora; she hasn't got the butterfly mark. So it must be you."

There was a tiny silence and Rose saw a flicker of pain pass across Thomas's face. It felt as if somebody had reached right inside her chest and was squeezing her heart tightly. She could hardly breathe. Had she found her real family? Could it be that she wasn't Rose Campion, but Rose Easingford? Suddenly the thought of no longer being Thomas's daughter and living at Campion's felt like a bereavement.

Aurora threw Rose an anxious look, and then she said quietly, "You're quite wrong, Lizzie. I do have a butterfly mark. But it's not on my neck, it's on my ankle. But you wouldn't know that because in all the years I lived with you, you never once bathed me, dressed me, never played with me or tickled me, never looked after me when I was sick, never cared for me at all."

She walked up to Lord Easingford. "Would you like me to show you my butterfly?"

He shrank away from her and Aurora said, "I may be an Easingford, but the only family I've ever known is the one I found with Rose and Thomas at Campion's." She put her arm through Rose's. "Rose Campion may not be my blood twin, but she will be my sister forever."

Several more policemen had arrived. They were attempting to pull the struggling Lizzie away.

"Wait," said Rose. She looked pleadingly at Lizzie. "Please. Tell me, where in the West End did you steal me from and what kind of pram was it?"

Lizzie laughed like a hyena.

"Oh, Rose, you don't know Lizzie Gawkin very well, do you? I make it a point never to give away information for free."

Lord Easingford stood weeping silently, his shoulders shuddering. A policeman approached him warily. "The gun, my lord," he said. "Please give me the gun."

Lord Henry was clearly a broken man. It was as if his entire face had, in the space of just a few minutes, cracked like the glaze on an expensive vase. He looked down at the pistol in his hand. He moved as if to hand it to the policeman and then he looked at Lizzie Gawkin, who was being led back down the street in handcuffs.

"Lizzie," he called. "Lizzie Gawkin." She turned and looked him straight in the face. "This is for my son," he said, and before anyone could stop him he shot her with an aim so true that the bullet hit her right in the middle of the forehead. Then he handed the still-warm gun to a policeman and said wearily, "Now, gentlemen, I'm ready to accompany you to the police station."

32

Rose, Thomas and Aurora stood at the end of the platform at Paddington Station. Although, Aurora wasn't so much standing as hopping from foot to foot and walking nervously around in circles while keeping one eye firmly fixed on the disembarking passengers. The boat train from Bristol bringing travellers from New York had arrived just a few minutes before in a cloud of steam, and porters in their blue uniforms with badges saying Great Western Railway were still scurrying around and piling trunks on to trolleys.

"Maybe he missed the train," said Aurora.

Rose squeezed her hand. She understood how Aurora must feel – when you long for something momentous to happen but also want to delay it because after it has happened there can be no going back to your old life.

"People are still coming down the platform," said Rose soothingly.

They were, but just a trickle now. A whistle was blown and the train at the next platform began moving with a judder and a screech. Steam billowed across the platform they were watching so intently. As the steam began to swirl and clear, a man could be just glimpsed walking from the far end of the platform towards them. He was holding a large battered leather holdall and his head was low. He drew nearer.

"There he is," said Rose.

"It may not be him," said Aurora in a small voice.

The man looked up. There could be no doubt. It was Edward Frederick Dorset, the new Lord Easingford. He looked so like Ned, and yet here in the flesh the resemblance to Aurora was unmistakable too. The man raised his head, faltered, stopped walking completely and stared at his daughter. A look of wonder and confusion crossed his face. Then he smiled shyly and raised a hand in a gesture that was part wave and part salute.

"Go on, Aurora," said Rose. "Go and meet your father. He's come all the way from America to see you."

Aurora looked uncertainly at Rose for a moment, and Rose whispered something and gave Aurora a little push to propel her down the platform towards Edward.

Thomas put his arm around Rose. She smiled up at him. "Don't look so worried, Thomas. I know what you're thinking. You're thinking that I'm watching and wishing it was me, wishing I'd found my father."

"And are you?" asked Thomas very gently. "It would be natural if you were."

Rose shook her head so her chestnut curls bobbed vigorously. "There was a tiny moment, no more than a second, on that ghastly night when I thought that I might be the lost child and I thought how wonderful it was to know for certain who you are and where you came from." What she didn't say was that in that same moment she had also seen the loss etched on Thomas's face.

Rose fingered the cuff of Thomas's greatcoat. "You'll always be my father, Thomas. Campion's will always be my home." She grinned. "And it's just as well that it turns out I'm not a lady, or I'd have had to go back to Miss Pecksniff's and that would have killed either her or me."

Thomas smiled down at her. "Whatever happens I'll always be there for you, Rose. Always. We'll ask the police for reports of babies snatched from prams in the West End thirteen years ago. It's more than we've ever had to go on in the past. Maybe we will find some trace of your parents. And I'm going to get Mr Cherryble to see if there is anything that might be done for little Effie's mother."

Aurora and Edward were walking towards Rose and Thomas together, unmistakably father and daughter. They were already chatting away as if they had known each other all their lives.

"Rosie," asked Thomas curiously, "what did you whisper to Aurora just now?"

Rose smiled. "I just told her that if she didn't like Edward Easingford she could always stay at Campion's with us, and you would be her father. After all, we are almost sisters."

Aurora and Edward had reached Rose and Thomas, and Edward put his hand out. "Mr Campion, I'm so pleased to meet you. Thank you for your letter. Getting the news that my daughter had been found has made me the happiest man alive."

"Thomas, your lordship. Call me Thomas."

Edward grinned. "You'd better drop the lordship too. I'm Ed. It's what my friends call me and I hope we will be fast friends, Thomas."

He turned to Rose. "And you must be the Rose that Lizzie Gawkin left on the steps along with Aurora."

Rose nodded. "And you're an actor. Just like Ned was."

"Poor Ned," said Edward. "To think that I found a cousin and lost him in the space of a few weeks. I feel as if I have lost a brother. Was he a good actor?"

"A good actor and a good man," said Rose softly.

Edward nodded. "He must have been. Without Ned I would never have found Aurora, my lost daughter."

"Are you a good actor, Ed?" asked Rose.

"I'm not sure it's for me to say. But I've done a fair bit. I had just left Chicago to play Hamlet in New York when the news reached me from Thomas and I left for England immediately."

"Goodness, Aurora," grinned Rose. "He really must love you very much to have sacrificed playing Hamlet in New York for you."

"Shall we go back to Campion's?" asked Thomas.

"Yes," said Aurora. "I want to show Edward everything. The best that Campion's Palace of Varieties and Wonders has to offer."

"And that includes our bicycle act," said Rose. "It's the hit of the season. We've had offers from all over, but we'll never do it anywhere but Campion's."

33

The trunks and cases were stacked up by the stage door ready to be taken by carriage to King's Cross Station and from there by train to Yorkshire. There was the first hint of spring in the air. Freddie was in the yard playing with Ophelia the cat. Already his new velvet knickerbockers were covered with mud.

Grace shook her head and smiled at Sarah Easingford, who was sitting on one of the trunks. The colour seemed to have come back into her eyes. Every day since she and Grace were released from the asylum she seemed more substantial as if she were a ghost coming back to life.

"I fear we're never going to make a gentleman out of Freddie," laughed Grace.

Sarah smiled. "In my experience, gentlemen are overrated."

Grace reached for Sarah's hand, and asked softly, "Are you nervous about returning to Easingford?"

"The past is the past," said Sarah. "I cannot change it. But I can make a future for myself. The loss of Edgar is unbearable, but I never really knew my son. He was taken from me when he was just a babe. Finding he had a family, finding you and my grandson, Freddie, are very great compensations. And then of course there is my great-niece, Aurora, in whom my poor dear sister lives on every day. And Edward, of course." She sighed. "I pity my dead husband. Poor Henry. They say he died of a heart attack, but I think what little heart he had left was broken by the knowledge that he'd brought such dishonour to the only thing he truly cared about: the ancient name of Easingford."

* ✳ *

Aurora, Edward, Thomas, Mr Cherryble and the new Lord Easingford's lawyer, Mr Merryfield, pushed back their chairs in Thomas's study and stood.

"I think that's the last of the papers that need

to be signed for now," declared Mr Merryfield, and he turned to Edward. "You are leaving for Easingford immediately?"

"Within the hour," said Edward, glancing at Aurora's pale face.

Mr Merryfield nodded. "You must be eager to see your birthright," he said.

Edward gave a non-committal grunt. "It will be strange seeing the place where I was born, and where I was supposed to have died." He rose. "Aurora, my dear one, I'm sure you want to say goodbye to your friends. Gentlemen, please come downstairs with me for a drink. I'll see you shortly, Aurora."

Edward and Thomas went downstairs together chatting like old friends. Thomas had already become a bit of a father figure to Edward, and Edward had insisted on giving Thomas an interest-free loan to secure Campion's future.

Aurora found Rose riding the bicycle up and down in the yard. Her eyes started brimming with tears. "I've only just found my Campion's family," she said, "and now I've got to get used to a whole new one."

"Edward's lovely," said Rose. "He reminds

me so much of Ned. And Thomas really likes him."

"He *is* very nice," said Aurora, "but I keep wondering when he will stop feeling like a stranger and start feeling like a father."

She looked apologetically at Rose. "I'm so sorry, Rose. I know I sound like I'm moaning. All I ever wanted was a real family and now I've got a ready-made one including a father, two aunts and a cousin, and yet it's surprisingly hard to get used to. And leaving Campion's and you and Effie and Thomas, and leaving doing our act and going to Easingford..." She trailed off.

"You should tell Edward how you feel," insisted Rose.

"But I don't want to seem ungrateful."

"I think a man who gave up playing Hamlet will understand," said Rose. "And in any case I think he probably already knows."

They found Edward sitting alone on the middle of the stage in the empty theatre.

"I love this stage," he said.

"We do too," said Rose.

"I can understand that," said Edward. "I've only been at Campion's a couple of weeks and already it feels like home."Aurora burst into tears.

"Aurora!" said Edward, jumping up and putting his arm around her. "Please don't cry. Listen, let's go to Easingford and take a look. And maybe Thomas will let us take Rose with us for a little holiday. And if it doesn't feel like home – well then, we'll come straight back here again. We can settle Sarah, Grace and Freddie in Yorkshire if that's what they all want, but there's no reason why you and I have to live at Easingford. If you want to come back to Campion's, I won't stop you. I promise."

"Do you really mean that?" asked Aurora.

"I'd never lie to you, Aurora; there have been too many lies in the past."

Edward looked at Rose. "Will you come with us for a week or two? If Thomas doesn't mind?"

"I'll be delighted to see the back of her for a bit," grinned Thomas, walking on to the stage to join them. "You'd better go and pack, Rosie, if you really are quite sure you want to go to the country. I went there once and it was horrible. Full of cows and sheep and so dark at night I thought I'd gone blind."

Rose and Aurora giggled. "They say that in

the country when there are no clouds you can see all the stars in the night sky," said Rose.

"You can see stars every night of the week at Campion's Palace of Varieties and Wonders, clouds or no clouds," replied Thomas tartly. "You don't have to go all the way to the ruddy country."

They all burst out laughing. Rose stood for a moment on the stage after the others had left to gather their belongings. She suddenly sensed movement in the gallery. She looked up and saw a ghostly figure. It was Ned. But he was much more insubstantial than he had been on previous sightings. He looked at her, smiled, mouthed the words, "Thank you" and disappeared. Rose knew she wouldn't see him again.

* ✳ *

The carriage rumbles along muddy, rutted Hangman's Alley. Just before they turn the corner, Rose and Aurora both lean out of the window to get one last glimpse of Campion's and of Thomas, Effie, Lottie, Molly, Jem and all the others, including O'Leary, who are standing outside waving goodbye. Rose knows she will hold the image of their wild, smiling, happy faces in her heart for the entire journey to Yorkshire. The carriage heads off alongside the silvery Thames. There is no fog today. The great river shimmers in the sunlight under an apricot sky. The mudlarks see Rose and Aurora through the open window and chase after the carriage, shouting. Rose takes Aurora's hand and squeezes it hard. As they clatter onward, Rose puts her head out of the carriage window to listen to the hum of London. The city and Campion's sing to her, a siren song calling her back.

Look out for the first title in
Lyn Gardner's *Olivia* series:

Olivia's First Term

LYN GARDNER

Turn the page for a sneak peek!

Chapter One

Olivia Marvell stood on the pavement in the pouring London rain. She screwed up her eyes as she lifted her face to the sky and the rain lashed down so hard it was like hundreds of tiny pinpricks. Olivia sighed. Even the weather had a grudge against her. She glanced at her dad, Jack, who since they had left the Tube station had been wrestling with an umbrella that kept being caught by the wind and turning itself inside out. The umbrella was clearly going to win. Jack looked as cold, wet and miserable on the outside as Olivia felt inside. She shivered. She hated London already; she had only been here for a few hours, and longed for the Italian late-summer sunshine that made you want to arch your back and stretch like a cat.

In one hand Olivia held a battered, bulging suitcase out of which poked a sodden, slightly muddy pyjama leg and the end of a thick wire; in the other she was holding the hand of Eel, her little sister. Eel hadn't been christened Eel, of course, but had acquired the nickname soon after birth because she was such a wriggly little thing, never still for a minute. She was jiggling around now, pulling on Olivia's hand, but Olivia only held on tighter.

"Cut it out, Eel! Anyone would think you were seven months old, not seven years," said Olivia irritably.

A few passers-by eyed them curiously, and one smartly dressed woman crossed over the road as if to avoid the raggle-taggle group.

"Bet she thinks that we're going to beg for money or mug her," muttered Olivia fiercely.

"You can't blame her," said Eel sadly, shaking her chestnut curls like a dog and spraying Olivia's face with more water. "We look rubbish. We probably pong too," she said, sniffing herself like a bloodhound. She was wrong about that, but they did look a mess. Olivia's hair was stuck damply to her face while Eel had a big smudge on her forehead and her skirt was torn after an unfortunate encounter with the ticket barriers at the Tube station. Eel had never seen ticket barriers before and had decided she never wanted to see them again. They had appeared determined to gobble her up.

"Come on, girls," said Jack, abandoning his tussle with the umbrella. "We'll be soaked through if we stand here any longer. Let's just walk fast. It's not very far." They set off at a brisk pace, even though it made Jack limp badly, and as they turned the corner of the street, an imposing red-brick building came into view. At the front of the building a sign written in large black letters declared "The Swan Academy of Theatre and Dance". In smaller letters below it said "An academic and performing arts education for talented children aged 7–16". Underneath that was written in italics: *"Proprietor: Alicia Swan"*.

"Here we are," said Jack, coming to a halt opposite the building and dragging them into a shop doorway for shelter.

Olivia's mouth fell open as she read the sign, and then she turned to her father and said accusingly, "It's a *stage* school. You said that we were going to stay with our grandmother and go to her school. You didn't tell us that she runs a *stage school*." Olivia spat out the words "stage school" as if they had a nasty taste.

Jack looked like a small boy who had just been caught with his fingers in the sweet jar. "Didn't I? I must have forgotten to mention it."

Olivia glared at him. "But you've always said that you hate all that fake theatre stuff, and so do we."

"Not me," piped up Eel. "I've always wanted to learn to dance but we've never stayed anywhere long enough to have lessons." She tried to do a little twirl and got tangled up with Olivia, who was still gripping her hand. "I'll be a great dancer. The bestest."

"You can't say bestest," said Olivia witheringly.

"I can if I want," said Eel, but she looked as if she might cry.

"I'm sure you'll be a fantastic dancer," said Jack soothingly, but Olivia detected a note of false cheerfulness in his tone.

"But what about me?" demanded Olivia. "I can't dance and I won't dance, and I don't want to go to stage school either. I want to stay with you and carry on walking the high-wire.

I'm a circus artist, not a stage-school brat."

Jack looked at his elder daughter, at her determined mouth and flashing eyes, and for a moment thought that his beloved wife, Toni, had suddenly come back to life. He shook his head sadly before swallowing hard and declaring a little too heartily, "Well, there is a choice. It's stage school or the orphanage run by a wicked old witch who eats children for breakfast."

"Well, I vote for stage school," said Eel, hopping from one leg to another, "and Livy will have to come too because she's superglued herself to me and is holding my hand so hard it hurts."

"That's because you can't be trusted!" said Olivia, the words exploding out of her mouth like a stuck cork suddenly released from the neck of a bottle. "It's all your fault that we're in this situation. If you hadn't. . ." She tailed off as she saw Eel and Jack's faces, white with shock. Olivia's anger evaporated as quickly as it had materialised and she burst into loud, guilty tears.

"Oh Eel, I didn't mean it! I'm really, really sorry," she sobbed. "I know it was an accident. It's just everything feels so miserable, and I'm tired of pretending everything is all right when it's not."

Eel hugged her and said tearfully, "It's OK, Livy. But we've got to make the best of things." She moved her head close to Olivia's and whispered, "We've got to be as brave as llamas and very cheerful. For Dad's sake, cos he hardly ever smiles now."

"I think you mean lions, Eel. Llamas probably aren't that brave. But you're right, Dad is so sad and defeated all the time." And, as if somebody had turned on a hosepipe, Olivia's tears started flowing again.

"He looks just like my teddy bear looked after he accidentally got put in the washing machine on an extra-hot wash," replied Eel sadly. "If it was an accident," she added ominously.

"It's nobody's fault," said Jack firmly. "We've just had some bad luck, my lovelies, but our luck will change."

"Look," said Eel, sniffing and pointing at the sky, "it's changing already. It's stopped raining and the sun has come out. I might even dry out if Livy would only stop crying all over me." Olivia gave a wan smile and hiccupped. . .